*A
Harlequin
Romance*

OTHER
Harlequin Romances

by BARBARA CUST

1588—THE LEAPING FLAME

SCENT OF THE MAQUIS

by

BARBARA CUST

Harlequin Books

TORONTO • LONDON • NEW YORK • AMSTERDAM • SYDNEY • WINNIPEG

Original hardcover edition published in 1976
by Mills & Boon Limited

ISBN 0-373-01982-3

Harequin edition published June, 1976

CHAPTER I

It wasn't until she was sitting in the airport departure
lounge with a cup of coffee on the table in front of her
that Marisa Farnham really faced up to the difficulties of
the task which lay before her. Then a wave of panic
swept over her and to combat it she picked up her cup,
only to have her elbow jogged as she did so with the
result that a stream of coffee flowed over the plastic-
topped table.

'Oh, I'm sorry,' said a voice behind her. 'It hasn't
touched your suit, has it? I'll get you another cup.'

A cloth was produced and the flood mopped up while
Marisa assured the girl who came back with another cup
of coffee that no damage had been done.

'I'm glad of that. You don't mind if I sit here, do you?
Most of the tables are full.'

The speaker was dark with long, shining hair and huge
brown eyes. She was wearing cream cotton slacks with a
loose scarlet shirt and her feet were bare in her cream
sandals in spite of the fact that outside there was a cool
breeze blowing over the airfield. A bulky cream bag was
slung over her shoulder and her fingers fiddled restlessly
with its metal clasp while there were shadows under her
eyes and a disconsolate droop to her mouth.

'Where are you going?' she asked abruptly.

'To Corsica,' answered Marisa. 'My flight to Bastia is
due to be called in about ten minutes.'

'That's my flight too. Where are you staying in
Corsica?'

'In Calvi.'

'So am I. At least I'm staying with my sister and her
brother-in-law in a villa just outside the town. Are you
on holiday?'

Marisa hesitated, then said firmly: 'Yes.'

'I'm not,' sighed the girl. 'That is, not entirely. I'm

supposed to be helping to look after my niece while getting over an unfortunate love affair. Leonie thinks that once I'm away from London I'll forget all about Martin, but she's quite wrong.'

She poured out these confidences with a complete lack of inhibition, and Marisa said fascinatedly: 'Leonie is your sister?'

'Yes, she—'

The girl, whose eyes were fixed on the double glass doors leading into the snack-bar, suddenly paled and then rose slowly to her feet. Marisa turned her head and saw a tall youth coming towards them, a boy who was dressed as casually as the girl.

'Martin,' she whispered, 'you've come! How did you know I'd be here?'

'Never mind that,' he flung at her savagely. 'Did you think I could bear the thought of our spending the whole summer apart?'

'But you said—'

'We both said a lot of damn silly things. Look, we must talk.'

At that moment the loudspeaker announced the departure of Flight 503 to Bastia and asked all passengers to proceed to Gate Nine. The boy and girl continued to gaze into each other's eyes, and Marisa said deprecatingly: 'The flight's been called, you know,' as she picked up her hand luggage.

'Oh, I can't go now,' declared the girl blithely. She smiled bewitchingly at Marisa. 'Will you do me a great favour and tell Blake what's happened?'

'But I don't know what's happened,' protested Marisa, 'and who's Blake?'

'Blake Wantage, Leonie's brother-in-law. Just say that Sue and Martin are together again and he'll understand.'

'But how will I recognise him?'

'He's tall and fair and he'll be at the airport to meet me; you can't miss him. Martin, my luggage, they'll be loading it on to the plane. We'd better be doing something about that.'

Without a backward glance the two of them rushed away, and as the announcement of the Bastia flight was repeated over the loudspeaker Marisa moved in the opposite direction. She made her way to Gate Nine and a short while later was seated in the aircraft, fastening her seat belt. She shivered as the plane hurtled along the runway and the noise of the engines rose to a crescendo. Now she was committed; she couldn't turn back.

It was only a month since her uncle's death, but it seemed like a lifetime. Two years of cooking, cleaning and nursing a partially paralysed man had come to an abrupt end when he didn't survive his second stroke, leaving her with very little more than the house in which she had been brought up and the knowledge that at last she was free to go in search of her brother Michael.

It was just over two years since he had stormed out of the house declaring that he never meant to come back and nine months since a letter, postmarked 'Calvi' but bearing no address, had arrived from him. She would have scraped together the money then to go to Corsica, but she couldn't leave her uncle. He was a hard man and insistent on having his own way, but he had taken Michael and herself into his home when their parents died and brought them up, little though he must have relished the task, since he was the complete bachelor and had nothing in common with a young niece and nephew. That was the root of the tragedy.

From the very beginning he and Michael had been in conflict. The boy, heartbroken and bewildered at the sudden loss of his parents in a road accident, had reacted by becoming sullen and unmanageable, and his uncle had made no allowance for his grief. He had sent Michael away to school, but Marisa had been allowed to attend the local grammar school and though her uncle ignored her for the most part the housekeeper he employed was a warmhearted woman, with the result that Marisa had grown up less deprived than her brother.

7

Unfortunately when Michael had left school his uncle had insisted on articling him to a firm of accountants. Michael loathed the work, and soon after his nineteenth birthday had had a blazing row with his uncle, after which he declared that he intended to make his own way in the world and disappeared. His uncle, furious at being defied, had worked himself up into such a rage that he suffered a stroke which had paralysed him down one side and robbed him of his speech.

Marisa, desolate at the loss of her brother, had left school at eighteen to run the house and look after her uncle with no time or money to spare to try to trace Michael's whereabouts. There had been only two communications from him. Neither gave an address, but the first one stated that he was well and in France, having joined the Foreign Legion, and the second from Corsica indicated that he was finding the life hard but that he didn't regret what he had done.

After her uncle's death Marisa discovered that everything had been left to her, though apart from the house which was three-storey Victorian and too big for the average family he had owned very little.

'If I can trace Michael I shall sell the house and hand over half the proceeds to him,' she told the solicitor.

'You're under no moral obligation to do that,' he pointed out.

'Perhaps not, but Michael has as much right to Uncle William's money as I have. I shall travel to Corsica, to Calvi where the second letter came from, and make some enquiries.'

'It may be a fruitless errand.'

'But that's the only clue I've got. I can't just sit here and do nothing. I've enough money to take a short holiday, so I shall go to a travel agent and ask him to fix me up with an air ticket and a hotel booking.'

But that was easier said than done. It was now July and the height of the season. Single rooms were at a premium on the island at any time, the travel agent told her, and in spite of all his efforts he had to report failure. He could book her a midweek flight, but he couldn't find her a hotel room anywhere in Calvi.

'Why not postpone your trip?' he suggested. 'I could fix you up in the second half of September or early October.'

'I must go now,' insisted Marisa.

The thought of waiting another two months was intolerable; besides, her resources were limited and she would need to get a job very soon. If she were to go in search of Michael it must be now, so recklessly she decided to book her flight and trust to finding accommodation when she reached Calvi. There had to be a room somewhere, she reasoned, even if it were only in a cottage, and on the spot it would be easier to find it.

That had seemed perfectly logical while she was still in England, but now she was in the plane with the end of her journey in sight she didn't feel nearly so confident. As she fastened her seat belt again, preparatory to landing, panic swept over her once more and this time it was more difficult to combat it.

The sun was blazing down as she emerged from the aircraft and crossed the tarmac. Inside the airport buildings a group of tourists milled round a courier, and Marisa wished that she had someone on whom she could dump her luggage and who would conduct her safely to her hotel. Then she stiffened her spine and exhorted herself to show some courage. If she were going to give way right at the beginning of her quest how could she hope to discover what had happened to Michael?

She waited for her luggage to appear, collected it and then turned to go in search of a taxi. As she did so she noticed a tall fair man glancing impatiently around and she remembered Sue. This must be Blake Wantage, she recognised the description, but he looked decidedly unapproachable. Still, there was no help for it; she couldn't let him hang round waiting for a girl who was remaining in London, so she took a deep breath and walked towards

9

him. He gave her an indifferent glance and then turned away, obviously concluding that she couldn't be intending to speak to him.

Tired and apprehensive, Marisa felt her temper rise, but she choked it down and enquired: 'Are you Mr. Wantage?'

'Yes,' he answered curtly.

Thinking that he couldn't be less helpful if he tried, Marisa ploughed on: 'Er—Sue was to have come on my flight, but at the last moment she changed her mind. She asked me to tell you that she and Martin are together again. She said you would understand what that meant.'

He said furiously: 'Of all the—! Are you a friend of hers?'

'Oh no, we only met at the airport. We shared a table in the snack-bar, and then just before our flight was called this boy arrived. I suppose he was Martin; anyway, Sue decided not to make the journey and asked me to tell you what had happened.'

'Typical of her to persuade someone else to do her dirty work for her.' With an effort Blake Wantage mastered his anger and said formally: 'Thank you, Miss—?'

'Farnham, Marisa Farnham.'

'Goodbye.'

He strode swiftly away and Marisa moved towards the exit, hoping that outside she would find a taxi to take her to Calvi. There was no sign of any vehicle, however, except a coach into which the tourists were climbing, and even as she looked round the last passenger being settled it rumbled away. She stared about her rather forlornly, deciding that she had better go back inside the building and make some enquiries about transport, when suddenly Blake Wantage appeared and walked towards a grey car.

He hadn't exactly endeared himself to her, but at least he spoke English, so on an impulse Marisa called: 'Mr. Wantage!'

He stopped and glanced back impatiently while his 'Yes?' was the reverse of encouraging.

'I—I wondered if you could tell me whether I could get a taxi to take me to Calvi.'

'Even if you could it would be very expensive,' he said uncompromisingly. 'It's a two and a half hour journey. Hasn't your hotel arranged to send a car for you?'

Marisa flushed. 'I—I haven't booked into a hotel. I'm going to look for accommodation when I reach Calvi.'

His eyebrows rose. 'I wish you luck.'

'I'll find something,' declared Marisa with much more confidence than she really felt.

'But first you have to get there.' He hesitated, then said with marked reluctance: 'I'm going back to Calvi myself, so I can give you a lift.'

It was painfully obvious that it was the last thing he wanted to do and it was humiliating to have to accept his offer, but Marisa couldn't afford to indulge her pride if it meant being stranded at the airport or having to pay out an enormous sum of money to persuade someone to take her into the town. She said stiffly: 'I'd be very grateful if you would,' and slid into the car as he took her suitcase from her and slung it into the back.

As they left the airport behind she noticed the many cypresses planted nearby and how close the mountains seemed. Their lower slopes were wooded, and as Blake Wantage drove along little streams zig-zagged through the trees to cool the air. The pungent shrubs which formed the *maquis* covered the hillside and scented the breeze which blew in through the open windows of the car, and Marisa drew in deep breaths of it.

Blake Wantage was almost completely silent on the journey, and Marisa judged that he preferred to concentrate on tackling the procession of hairpin bends which separated Bastia from Calvi so refrained from starting a conversation herself. When eventually they reached Ile-Rousse he remarked: 'Only another fifteen miles to go. I expect you're getting tired.'

'A little,' admitted Marisa. 'I was up early this morning.'

He shot her a keen glance and she was aware that she must be looking rather travel-stained by now. The beige Trevira trouser suit which complemented her soft chestnut hair and hazel eyes had one or two dark smudges on it and the green and stone striped shirt which had looked so crisp and fresh when she set out was wilting.

She quailed at the thought of touring Calvi to search for accommodation, and perhaps something of this showed in her face, because her companion said abruptly: 'I'll take you to the villa I'm sharing with my sister-in-law so that you can have a cool drink and a rest before I drive you into Calvi.'

'I couldn't put you to all that trouble,' protested Marisa. 'If you'll take me straight to Calvi and drop me there I shall be quite all right.'

'Nonsense,' he answered brusquely, and drove on as if that settled the matter.

In spite of her fatigue Marisa seethed at this treatment, and when they eventually turned into the gateway of a dazzlingly white villa she longed to be able to pick up her luggage and stalk away without a backward glance. Since this was out of the question she gritted her teeth and followed Blake Wantage into a cool tiled hall and then through a sitting-room on to a terrace shaded with vines. Steps led from this down to a pool where a strikingly lovely dark-haired woman lay stretched out on a scarlet canvas chair. She was wearing a matching scarlet bikini and at the edge of the pool a dark-haired little girl played with a pile of pebbles.

The woman on the lounger turned her head to say: 'So you're back, Blake,' then sat up. 'Who's this, and where's Sue?'

'Sue has decided to stay in England,' answered Blake Wantage grimly. 'She left Miss Farnham, who was travelling on the same plane, to inform me of this, which was extremely considerate of her since otherwise I should have still have been kicking my heels at the airport wondering what had become of her. Leonie, this is Miss Marisa Farnham. Miss Farnham, my sister-in-law, Mrs. Wantage. Sit down while I go in search of drinks.'

Uncomfortably aware of the other woman's appraising glance, Marisa sat down on a nearby chair.

'How utterly maddening of Sue,' said Leonie Wantage crossly. 'She knew that I was counting on her to help to look after Fiona. I didn't realise that she'd arranged to travel out with anyone. Have you known her long?'

'I don't know her at all,' explained Marisa. 'We shared the same table in the airport buffet, then before the flight was called this young man rushed up and your sister decided not to make the journey after all.'

'The man would be Martin Appledore. He and Sue have been conducting an on-off affair for the past six months, but I thought everything was definitely over between them. That's why Sue agreed to come out here for the summer and lend a hand with Fiona.'

It was obvious that Leonie Wantage was extremely put out, and Marisa felt unwelcome. She was reduced to wishing that Blake Wantage would come back even though his high-handedness annoyed her when Fiona scrambled to her feet, tripped over the heap of pebbles and plunged into the pool. She uttered a terrified scream and Marisa, expecting the mother to dive in to the child's rescue, was appalled when Leonie Wantage, having leaped out of her chair, did nothing but wring her hands and cry distractedly: 'Blake, Blake, where are you? Fiona's drowning!'

She rushed towards the villa just as Fiona, choking and gasping, came to the surface, and Marisa, kicking off her sandals, wasted no more time but dived into the pool. In a few swift strokes she reached Fiona, and grabbing the little girl steered her to the side, then lifted her out of the water. Fiona was crying and shivering with shock and fright, so picking her up in her arms, Marisa ran on to the terrace just as Blake Wantage appeared with Leonie

13

behind him.

'Give her to me,' he ordered, and relieved of her burden, Marisa stood there, dripping with water and wondering what to do next.

'Thank goodness you can swim,' cried Leonie. 'I can't, so it was no use my jumping into the pool. Come into my bedroom and take off those wet things while I find you something to wear.'

Marisa padded after her into a luxuriously furnished bedroom with a wardrobe fitment lining the whole of one wall. Leonie slid back the doors to pull out a pair of white slacks and a yellow shirt.

'I think these should fit you,' she said. 'You can dry yourself in the bathroom next door and leave your clothes there.'

There were pale pink fluffy towels to match the pale pink fitments in the adjoining bathroom, and Marisa was soon warm and dry again. Leonie's clothes, together with the bra and pants she provided, were a reasonable fit, though the slacks were a little short in the leg, and emerging into the bedroom again, Marisa tidied her hair, which was drying rapidly, before making her way downstairs.

Blake Wantage was waiting for her in the hall to enquire: 'Are you all right? Come and have a brandy and some hot coffee.'

'I don't need either,' Marisa assured him. 'I'm not suffering from shock since it was certainly no hardship to plunge into the water on such a hot day. How is Fiona?'

'None the worse now that she's got over her fright, but Leonie's put her to bed.'

'I'm glad I happened to be there. Your sister-in-law tells me she can't swim.'

'All the more reason why she should keep her eye on Fiona,' commented Blake Wantage exasperatedly.

'I gathered that was to be Sue's job,' said Marisa as they sat down on the terrace and he poured out a cup of coffee for her.

14

'Yes,' he answered uncommunicatively, and looked at his watch.

Feeling snubbed, she said immediately: 'As soon as I've drunk this I must be off. Perhaps I could get hold of a taxi to take me into Calvi. I could leave my wet clothes here and pick them up tomorrow.'

'A far better idea would be for you to have dinner here and stay the night, then tomorrow morning you'll feel more like searching for accommodation.'

'Oh no, that would be too inconvenient for you.'

'The obligation's all on our side,' said Blake Wantage formally. 'If you hadn't been at hand Fiona would have drowned.'

'If you hadn't gone for a drink for me you would have been there to rescue her,' pointed out Marisa.

'Let's just agree that a good night's rest wouldn't do you any harm, shall we?' he countered dryly, and as Leonie emerged from the villa he stood up.

'If you'll excuse me I've some work to do. I'll see you at dinner.'

There didn't seem any point in protesting further, and Marisa admitted to herself that she wasn't looking forward to walking round Calvi this evening in search of a lodging for the night. She was more tired than she had realised and the coffee had been just what she needed.

Leonie dropped into a chair, saying: 'Fiona's asleep, I'm thankful to report. She has so much energy that she wears me out. At home I have an au pair to look after her, but the current girl's gone back to Sweden, which was one of the reasons I decided to join Blake when he was offered the use of this villa for the summer.'

'I thought perhaps it belonged to you.'

'Heavens no, I wish it did. It belongs to the head of Blake's firm whose wife was a Frenchwoman. She came into possession of this piece of land in Corsica and persuaded her husband to build a villa on it, but unfortunately she died before she could really enjoy it.'

Leonie stopped and hesitated, then went on: 'Blake

15

suggested that you should stay the night and I agreed with him. We've two spare rooms, so it would be no trouble at all.'

'If you're quite sure of that then I'll accept the invitation. I must admit that I don't feel much like going down to Calvi now and enquiring for a room tonight.'

'I'm certain you don't, so that's settled. Unfortunately I counted on Sue being here this evening, so I arranged to go out and I haven't been able to cancel it. I was wondering if in the circumstances you could keep an eye on Fiona for me. She's fast asleep and there's no reason at all for her to wake, but if she should you'd be at hand. You see, Blake won't be in the house. There's a studio in the garden where he works, so he wouldn't hear her if she should call or have a bad dream. There is a housekeeper living in with her husband who is the gardener-cum-handyman, but she isn't very good with children. There'd be no need for you to stay up; you could sleep in the room next to Fiona's.'

Marisa was perfectly ready to agree; it would be one way of repaying the hospitality extended to her.

'Certainly I'll listen out for her. I'm a light sleeper and should hear her if she's restless.'

'Thank you so much.' Leonie looked immensely relieved. 'Now I'll show you your room and then tell Marie there'll be one extra for dinner.'

The bedroom was cool and uncluttered with a tiled floor and white walls. The curtains and bedcover had a sprigged pattern of green and white and there was a tiny green and white bathroom adjoining. They peeped into the next room where Fiona lay asleep, and then Leonie said: 'I'll leave you to come down again when you're ready. Go into the sitting-room and help yourself to a drink.'

Marisa tidied herself, decided that it wasn't worth unpacking anything but the barest necessities, and eventually made her way downstairs to the sitting-room. There was a pile of new magazines on a table, so selecting one,

16

she was soon absorbed in it and was almost taken by surprise when Leonie appeared, wearing a black chiffon dress cut extremely low and enhancing every curve of her delightful figure.

'I shan't have time to change later,' she explained airily. 'Roger's calling for me immediately after dinner.'

There was no mention of her own husband and Marisa wondered if she were a widow or whether she was divorced, but decided that it was none of her business. Once she had left the villa the next day she didn't expect to see either of the Wantages again, particularly as their circumstances were very different from hers.

Leonie poured herself an aperitif, then walked across to the open french windows to stare out over the garden.

'I do hope Blake hasn't forgotten the time,' she said frowningly. 'Marie gets so cross if she can't serve the food the moment it's ready. Oh, good, here he is.'

He entered the room from the terrace and his eyebrows rose as he saw his sister-in-law.

'I don't flatter myself that that outfit's for my benefit,' he commented sarcastically. 'I take it you're spending the evening elsewhere.'

'But of course. I'm quite content to lie in the sun all day, but you must admit that it's desperately boring here in the evening.'

'And Fiona?'

'Miss Farnham has very kindly offered to keep an ear open for her. You know yourself that once she's asleep Fiona never wakes until morning. But do let's go in to dinner or everything will be ruined.'

They ate egg mayonnaise, veal with tiny browned potatoes, a green salad and vanilla ice cream covered with hot chocolate sauce followed by fresh pears. Leonie said: 'If you want coffee, Blake, you'll have to make it yourself. I haven't time and Marie and Jean are taking the rest of the evening off.'

The door bell rang and she jumped up to answer it. They heard her say: 'I'm quite ready, Roger, I'll just collect a wrap,' and then a man sauntered into the room.

He was tanned, his hair a close cap of curls framing his head, and his white teeth widened into an approving grin as his gaze took in Marisa.

'You're not very like your sister, are you?' he said casually, and she realised that he had taken her for Sue.

'I'm not—' she began, and then Blake Wantage cut in with: 'Leonie's sister wasn't able to come. This is Miss Farnham who is staying the night here and going on to Calvi tomorrow.'

His tone was quite even, but Marisa sensed his dislike of the newcomer who said: 'Since I've not been introduced, I'm Roger Dacre.' He raised his voice. 'Leonie, are you coming or not? At this rate and in my rattletrap we shan't reach Calvi until midnight.'

'Darling, don't be so impatient.' Leonie appeared with a black and crimson silk shawl over her shoulders and the two of them went out together calling: 'Good night.' Marisa began to collect the dishes and Blake Wantage said abruptly: 'Leave those. I'll carry them into the kitchen and Marie will see to them in the morning.'

'I'll help you clear away,' offered Marisa, and together they carried the dirty china into the kitchen to stack it by the sink.

'Do you want coffee?' enquired Blake Wantage. 'If so perhaps you'd like to make yourself a cup. I must go and do some work. I've wasted practically the whole day as it is.'

He disappeared without more ado, leaving Marisa feeling guilty and resentful at one and the same time. It wasn't her fault that he'd made the trip to Bastia for nothing. No wonder his sister-in-law preferred to go out for the evening! It wouldn't have been much fun for her if she had stayed in.

Because she couldn't think what else to do with her time Marisa began to wash up the dinner dishes. The kitchen was modern with plastic-topped working surfaces and two stainless steel sinks, so she had soon finished her

18

task. By that time the thought of a cup of coffee was attractive and she felt she had earned it, so she ground the beans she found in a jar next to the electric coffee mill and soon had the percolator bubbling. There was far too much coffee for one person; perhaps Mr. Wantage would enjoy a cup. She looked across the garden to where she could see a glimmer of light through the bushes. Should she take a tray of coffee to him or not? If he didn't want it he could always leave it.

She filled an earthenware pot she found in a cupboard and laid a tray, then set out across the garden with it. Beyond the bushes stood a small brick building, obviously a studio, and making for this she knocked on the door. It opened suddenly and Blake Wantage stood framed in the doorway.

'What do you want?' he demanded uncompromisingly.

'I made some coffee and thought you might like a cup.'

'What I would like more than anything,' he said bitingly, 'is not to be disturbed.'

Marisa flushed scarlet. 'I'm sorry, I didn't think——'

'That's the trouble. Women don't. Now go back to the villa and amuse yourself with the television or go to bed, but don't interrupt me again unless the house is on fire.'

The door closed and Marisa was left to carry her rejected offering back to the villa. She was trembling with anger and humiliation, conscious that it would have given her great satisfaction to have poured the pot of coffee over Mr. Wantage's head. She had never met a man with such appalling manners, and the sooner their ways divided the better she would like it. She dumped the tray in the kitchen and went upstairs to bed, to lie there tossing restlessly until she heard Leonie come home in the early hours of the morning.

As a result of this she slept later than she intended and was finally roused by Leonie coming into the bedroom with a tray holding a pot of coffee, croissants fresh from the baker, curls of butter and apricot jam.

'You shouldn't be waiting on me,' protested Marisa

19

guiltily. 'I usually wake much earlier, but I was a long time getting off.'

'I'm always the same the first night in a strange bed,' declared Leonie, 'and I brought your breakfast in because I want a word with you in private.'

She poured out two cups of coffee and went on: 'Have you any particular reason for wanting to stay in Calvi itself? I know you haven't fixed up any accommodation there and it struck me that if your object was to spend a few weeks pleasantly and cheaply in Corsica you might consider remaining here.'

'But I couldn't—you wouldn't want a stranger in the house—'

'I would if she'd agree to help with Fiona,' stated Leonie frankly. 'I'm not good with children and her interminable questions get on my nerves. When I agreed to spend the summer at the villa I thought Sue would be here to play nursemaid; I didn't bargain for having to cope with Fiona by myself.'

Marisa hesitated. 'I don't think Mr. Wantage would exactly welcome my presence here. He doesn't seem to have a very high opinion of women.'

'Oh, you don't need to bother about Blake,' returned Leonie carelessly. 'You'd scarcely see anything of him. He'll be spending all his time working in the studio.'

'Is he a painter?'

'No, an architect. His firm has been commissioned to design a combined shopping centre and leisure complex in a new town, and Blake's been given three months leave to draw up the plans. As I told you this villa belongs to his boss who suggested that Blake should come out here where he could concentrate without the distractions of life in town, and since I'd had a bad dose of 'flu in the spring Jon, my husband and Blake's brother, suggested that Fiona and I should join him to spend a summer in the sun. Sue had just declared that she and Martin were finished for ever, so she decided to come too, but since she had to work out a week's notice at her job she was to travel yesterday. Instead Blake turned up with you, so you see you're definitely the answer to my prayers.'

Again Marisa hesitated. She was reluctant to confide her plans for tracing Michael to Leonie Wantage, but it did occur to her that staying at the villa would give her much more time to carry them out. If she had to pay for accommodation she couldn't afford to stay in Corsica for more than a fortnight and it might be impossible to make much headway in that time. She had no experience of looking after children, but using plenty of patience and common sense it shouldn't be difficult to cope with Fiona.

She said: 'Providing I can get to Calvi in my spare time I'd like to accept your offer.'

'No need to worry about that, you can borrow one of the cars, either mine or Blake's. You do drive, I suppose?'

'Oh, yes,' said Marisa.

'Good. I couldn't pay much, but then you wouldn't expect more than pocket money living as a member of the family, would you?'

The sum Leonie named was certainly modest, but that didn't trouble Marisa, who was only too thankful to have a comfortable base from which to work.

Looking pleased with herself, Leonie stood up and said: 'I'll leave you to finish your breakfast and then you can unpack properly. I'll tell Blake that you're staying on and that he doesn't need to make that trip into Calvi this morning. That will please him, I'm sure.'

Marisa soon disposed of the coffee and croissants, then had a quick bath before unpacking her case. She put on cotton slacks and a sleeveless shirt to make her way out into the garden where Leonie was already ensconced by the pool.

'Hallo,' she said. 'I wonder if you'd mind going in search of Fiona? She's probably in the kitchen, but I don't want to tax Marie's patience too far. She and her husband Jean are employed by the Lamberts and they act as caretakers when the villa is empty. These Corsicans are horribly independent. Marie seems to think she's conferring a favour on me by agreeing to work here at all.'

'I'll bring Fiona out here,' said Marisa, and went back into the villa.

Fiona was in the kitchen, boredly diving under the table and out again much to Marie's fury.

'*Allez-vous-en!*' she hissed, breaking into a torrent of French as Marisa appeared which was so rapid that it was incomprehensible.

Fiona stood staring suspiciously at Marisa, and as the girl bent to take her hand she snatched it away.

'Go with Mademoiselle,' ordered Marie, waving a ladle menacingly. 'I do not want you here.'

Fiona's mouth puckered, and Marisa, feeling intensely sorry for the child who was in everyone's way, said coaxingly: 'Let's go into the garden and play a game.'

'Don't want to,' retorted Fiona stubbornly, but she turned and ran out of the kitchen with Marisa following.

Once in the garden the child halted to say aggressively: 'I want to play hide and seek, and I'll hide.'

'Very well,' agreed Marisa, and Fiona scampered away, crying: 'You'll never find me!'

They played until even Fiona was hot and tired, causing her mother to say shudderingly: 'I don't know how you can gallop about like that in the sun.'

'I'm thirsty,' complained Fiona. 'I want some orange juice; can I have some orange juice?'

'Certainly, if Miss Farnham will get it for you,' yawned her mother, 'and at the same time ask Marie to bring out a pot of coffee.'

Marie muttered darkly when asked to provide the coffee, and Marisa said: 'I'll make it myself if you don't mind my using the percolator.'

Marie's only answer was a shrug, so Marisa made the coffee, found orange juice in the fridge and carried a tray out to the pool. Fiona skipped beside her, and immediately the orange juice was drunk said: 'Now we'll play hide and seek again.'

22

Marisa shook her head. 'No, it's too hot. Wouldn't you like to swim in the pool?'

'Don't like the water,' muttered Fiona, ' 'cept when Uncle Blake holds me up.'

'If I showed you how to swim,' remarked Marisa casually, 'you wouldn't need anyone to hold you up. Come along and we'll find your swimsuit.'

When they came out to the pool again Leonie had disappeared and Fiona plumped down on to the chair her mother had been occupying, her face creased in fear.

'Don't want to go in,' she whimpered.

'Then you don't need to,' answered Marisa reassuringly. 'Sit on the side and watch me swim.'

She dived into the pool and swam two lengths, revelling in having it to herself. Swimming was one of her few accomplishments and she had won a bronze medal for it at school. She was making for the side where Fiona was sitting when a voice said dryly: 'Very professional!'

Marisa bit her lip at the sarcasm. She had been unaware of Blake Wantage's appearance, and the knowledge that he suspected her of showing off galled her. She climbed out of the pool and said stiffly: 'I was hoping gradually to persuade Fiona to join me and overcome her nervousness.'

'I'll come in with you, Uncle Blake,' Fiona decided maddeningly, but he answered firmly: 'Not this morning, chicken, I'm busy, and Miss Farnham can swim much better than I can.' He turned to Marisa. 'Leonie tells me you're staying on here in Sue's place to give her a helping hand.'

'Yes, she asked me to, and since I want to live near Calvi for a while it suits me very well. I presume you've no objection, Mr. Wantage?'

It was said challengingly, but she was quite unprepared for him to answer frowningly: 'Every objection. I don't approve of the idea at all.'

CHAPTER II

Marisa stared at him incredulously.

'But why?' she stammered. 'I mean—if you want references I could supply some from England, but I didn't suppose—'

'I'm not impugning your character,' he interrupted impatiently, 'but there's no necessity for anyone to be employed here to look after Fiona.'

'Your sister-in-law seems to think there is, and after all, her sister—'

Marisa allowed her voice to trail away significantly, and Blake Wantage's eyes narrowed in annoyance.

'Sue was coming here primarily to suit her own ends.'

'And I'm staying here for the same reason,' countered Marisa. 'It's your sister-in-law and not you who is employing me, Mr. Wantage.'

She saw his mouth harden, but he managed to control his temper.

'I don't know what your business is in Calvi, but I recommend you to finish it as soon as possible and go home.'

He strode away from the pool, leaving Marisa fuming at his high-handedness, but she swallowed her chagrin as she finally managed to coax Fiona into the water and actually attempt a few strokes. Then praising the little girl extravagantly she whisked her out of the water and kept her occupied until lunch.

After lunch Fiona took a nap, but both Leonie and Blake Wantage had vanished, so Marisa felt obliged to remain in the villa garden to take charge of Fiona when the little girl woke up. It was late afternoon when Leonie returned in the car, and evidently her conscience pricked her, because she said: 'I'm going out to dinner, Marisa, so I'll be obliged if you'll stay in, but you can have the whole morning off tomorrow, and as Jean is going into

Calvi to get some supplies he can give you a lift to the town.'

Marisa was relieved to hear this. She had begun to fear that this job would give her no chance at all to pursue her enquiries, but a free morning should provide the opportunity she was looking for. She spent a solitary evening with a pile of French magazines and went to bed early. Blake Wantage didn't even appear at dinner, and she saw Marie carrying a tray to the studio.

The next morning she accompanied Jean, Marie's husband, in the Renault which he drove into Calvi to park close to the Citadel. She stared up at the great bastion of rock where she had already discovered from him the Foreign Legion were stationed in the fort, deciding that her first move must be to walk up there and observe the place. Accordingly she arranged to return to the car in a couple of hours, leaving Jean to collect the various goods Marie had instructed him to buy and to visit his favourite bar.

The entrance to the Citadel was steep, and climbing the flight of cobbled steps which led into the old town she was glad to be wearing low-heeled sandals. She made her way towards the fort, and stopped as close to it as she could without attracting attention. It was a grim-looking place with its narrow slitted windows, the lower ones barred, and the small entrance door within the large one reminded her of television pictures she had seen of prisons. Had Michael been happy inside those stone walls or had he longed unceasingly for home and England?

Now that she was here she was at a loss to know what to do next. There was a bar nearby and she sat down at one of the iron tables in front of it to order a drink. When it came she sipped the Dubonnet slowly, hoping that it would give her inspiration. Since she was actually in Calvi she must do something—but what?

Her eyes fixed on the fort, she noticed legionnaires emerging from it in ones and twos, and wondered desperately if she could go to the gate and ask to see the commanding officer. Two of the legionnaires sauntered towards the bar and gave her an appreciative glance as they passed inside. They looked smart in their well-pressed khaki drill slacks and shirts, their sleeves rolled up and their képis on their heads, and she watched them greet the proprietor. Could she possibly speak to them and ask them if they knew of a Michael Farnham?

Trying to pluck up her courage, she ordered another Dubonnet before fixing her eyes on them. One of them stared back boldly at her and she flushed uncomfortably. She wanted to get up and walk away, but if she did how was she ever to make any progress in her quest?

The darker of the two men said something to his companion and they moved out of the bar to walk towards Marisa's table. She swallowed hard and tried to marshal her schoolgirl French into an enquiry about her brother. The legionnaires approached and one smiled at her, saying: '*Bonjour, mademoiselle*, you will take an aperitif with us?'

'No, thank you,' stammered Marisa, 'but I wondered if you could help me?'

'But of course.'

The darker one's smile was now definitely impudent, but Marisa tried to ignore this as she said haltingly: 'I am looking for my brother who joined the Legion about two years ago. His name is Michael Farnham, and I know that he was sent here to Calvi, but I have not heard from him for more than six months. Is it possible that you have come across him?'

Both legionnaires shrugged, and the darker one said: 'Possible, *mademoiselle*, but I do not recognise the name.'

'Is there any way in which I could find out where he is?'

Another shrug and then the darker one moved closer to her and put his hand caressingly on her arm.

'Perhaps we could discuss this over a little drink,' he suggested. 'It is a pity for such a pretty girl to be distressed.'

Marisa moved her arm sharply and realised how stupid

she had been.

She got up quickly, but the second legionnaire who had not spoken so far said: 'Why concern yourself about a brother? You will find it far more amusing with us, *mademoiselle*. We can give you a good time,' and his arm came round to encircle her waist.

She retreated from him, but the other man was standing so close to her that she began to feel frightened. Holding on to her courage, she said: 'Thank you, but I must go now,' and tried to edge past them.

The darker one's expression became almost menacing, and he said jeeringly: 'You don't think that we are good enough for you, eh, *mademoiselle*?'

'No, it's not that,' began Marisa, and then to her infinite relief a voice said: 'Hallo, Marisa, were you tired of waiting for me?' and she saw Roger Dacre coming towards them.

Her two companions exchanged glances, the darker one shrugged for the third time, and they moved away.

Marisa said thankfully: 'Oh, I'm so glad to see you! I didn't know how to get rid of them,' and Roger Dacre grinned.

'I don't often get such an enthusiastic welcome, but I thought even from a distance that you looked in need of a knight errant. Were they making a nuisance of themselves?'

'Well, I did rather encourage them by staring at them so hard,' admitted Maria. 'It was stupid of me to think they might be able to help me.'

'Help you?'

'To trace my brother.' She hadn't meant to confide in anyone, but suddenly it was out.

Roger looked at her sympathetically. 'Come along, join me in some coffee and tell me all about it. I haven't had any breakfast yet, so I can eat while we talk.'

Marisa sat down again while he walked into the bar, spoke to the proprietor and then joined her again.

'I always breakfast here,' he said, 'and it was lucky that

27

I was later than usual getting up today. Ah, here comes the coffee. Now pour it out and let me hear the whole story.'

Haltingly she told him about Michael, her uncle, and the situation she now found herself in.

'I do realise that it was stupid of me to approach those men, but I felt I couldn't go back to the villa without having made some progress. Do you know anyone who could find out where Michael is now?'

Roger looked thoughtful. 'I've only been living here a few months and though I've some acquaintances in the town I don't know anyone from the fort. Have you spoken to Blake Wantage? This isn't the first time he's been to Corsica and he moves in a higher social sphere than I do. He might know someone useful.'

'Oh, I don't want to trouble him,' answered Marisa quickly, and Roger grimaced.

'Too high and mighty for your taste, is he? Me too. I can't understand how Leonie came to have such a toffee-nosed brother-in-law.'

Although she didn't like Blake herself Marisa felt a curious reluctance at discussing him with Roger, so she said quickly: 'I ought to be getting back to the car. I don't want to keep Jean waiting.'

'I'll walk down with you,' and Roger accompanied her to the foot of the Citadel.

'I'll make a few enquiries,' he told her, 'to see if I can pick up any information about your brother. If I find anything out I'll let you know.'

Jean came up as they were speaking, so Marisa broke off the conversation and saying goodbye to Roger took her place in the car. Jean's English was good and he chatted freely about the island as he drove her back to the villa. Already she had decided that she much preferred him to his wife.

After lunch she spent the afternoon amusing Fiona and coaxing the little girl into the pool. By now Fiona had more confidence in the water, and Marisa hoped that before she left Corsica she would have succeeded teaching her to swim. Having seen her charge to bed she changed into a long cotton skirt and a brief ribbed top before walking through the sitting-room on to the terrace where Leonie was stretched out in a cane chair.

'Did you enjoy what you saw of Calvi this morning?' asked Leonie carelessly.

She had been missing most of the day, and when Marisa had arrived back at the villa Fiona had said that Mummy had gone out in the car.

'Very much. There wasn't really time to do more than take a look at the Citadel.'

'All by yourself?'

Something in Leonie's voice warned Marisa, and she answered cautiously: 'Chiefly, but I was having a drink at a café table when Roger Dacre came up.'

'Jean mentioned to Marie that Roger brought you back to the car.'

'It was pure coincidence that I happened to choose the café where apparently he breakfasts every day.'

'How remarkable!'

Marisa had the uncomfortable feeling that Leonie didn't believe her, but at that moment Blake Wantage came into the room and for the first time Marisa was glad to see him. She thought he looked tired and that it was an obvious effort for him to make polite conversation, so that altogether dinner was a silent meal since Leonie didn't chatter as much as usual.

They had just reached the cheese and fruit stage when the telephone rang and Marie came in to announce that the call was for Mademoiselle.

'For me?' queried Marisa in surprise. 'But I don't know anyone here.'

'You know one person,' said Leonie significantly, and Marisa bit her lip.

Leonie was right. It was Roger, and he greeted her cheerfully with: 'Well, I've been sleuthing all afternoon, but I haven't found anything out. How long is it since you heard from your brother?'

'About nine months.'

'The trouble is that recruits only stay in Corsica for six months and then they're posted somewhere else, so that anyone who was serving with your brother will probably have left the island now.'

'Oh, I see.' Marisa couldn't conceal her disappointment, and Roger said sympathetically: 'I'll continue to ask around, but I'm not very hopeful of gathering information. I really do think that your best bet is Blake Wantage. His boss who owns the villa had a Corsican wife and is very well in with all the local people, so I'm sure Wantage could pull a few strings for you.'

'Yes, I see. Thank you for what you've done, Roger, but I must go now. We're in the middle of dinner.'

'Right. See you soon.'

Marisa went slowly back to the dining-room and Leonie said sharply: 'What a long time you've been, but perhaps it was a very interesting conversation.'

She was plainly annoyed, and Marisa saw that there was nothing for it but to reveal why she had come to Corsica. If Blake Wantage could help her it was stupid to allow her pride to stand in the way.

She said: 'As you guessed, that was Roger Dacre. He's been trying all day to find out my brother's whereabouts for me, but without success.'

'Your brother's in Corsica?' queried Leonie in surprise.

'He was some months ago,' and Marisa went on to explain once more what had brought her to the island.

Blake Wantage said: 'If he was actually here in the Legion it must be possible to trace him. I don't know the commandant personally, but I can contact him.'

'I'd be very grateful if you would,' murmured Marisa. She was reluctant to put herself under an obligation to Mr. Wantage, but it was obvious that she wasn't going to get very far on her own and Roger didn't know the right people.

Blake Wantage excused himself, and left the two

women to drink their coffee. Marisa braced herself to endure a spate of questions about Michael from Leonie, but she needn't have worried. Leonie was too self-centred to take much interest in any subject which didn't concern herself, and immediately asked Marisa's opinion of Roger.

'Very good company,' answered Marisa cautiously. 'I was really glad to see him this morning when he came to my rescue.'

'Yes, two Frenchmen bent on conquest can be disconcerting when you're not experienced in handling men,' answered Leonie rather patronisingly. 'Funnily enough I met Roger in a similar place. The day after I arrived here I was having a drink in a café on the sea-front at Calvi and there was a sudden shower of rain. A lot of people dived inside the café to take shelter, among them Roger. He asked if the vacant seat at my table was taken, I said it wasn't, so he sat down.'

'What does he do for a living?'

'He's a freelance journalist, writing travel articles for magazines and supplementing his income by giving English lessons. He doesn't make a lot of money, but he does have fun. That day we met we started talking and I asked him what there was to do in Calvi, so he offered to show me the best night spots. Since then we've gone about quite a lot together.'

'Doesn't your husband mind?'

Leonie shrugged. 'He isn't here, is he, and he can't expect me to remain as cloistered as a nun. That's the trouble with Jon. He's an old stick-in-the-mud, wedded to his work in a merchant bank, and can't appreciate the fact that most of the time I'm so bored I could scream. He thinks a nice house and a child should be enough to occupy any woman. Both the Wantage men are rather feudal in their outlook. I pity the woman who marries Blake, but of course Giselle is well able to look after herself.'

Marisa wondered who Giselle was, but didn't have to wait long to find out.

Leonie went on: 'Royce Lambert is the senior partner in Blake's firm and Giselle is his daughter. He owns this villa and he and Giselle will be coming out later on to stay for a while. Blake and she have known each other for some years, and he spent a holiday here last summer. In a way I'm surprised he hasn't married Giselle before this, but I suppose he wants to be able to distinguish himself first so as to be able to offer her a good life. Of course she isn't without money of her own, her mother left her some, but Blake's not the type to live off his wife.'

Leonie stopped suddenly and said half-guiltily: 'Forget I told you all that, will you? Blake wouldn't thank me for discussing his private affairs.'

'I shan't mention them to anyone,' Marisa assured her, and when she went to bed found herself lying awake to speculate on what the unknown Giselle was like until she turned over and firmly fixed her thoughts on something else.

Two days went by in which she saw very little of Blake Wantage, and when she did he never mentioned Michael. She couldn't bring herself to ask him if he were making any progress in his enquiries, and her spirits sank lower and lower. It didn't help either that she caught only the merest glimpse of Roger, who was whisked away by Leonie the moment he showed his nose inside the villa. Marisa spent her time amusing Fiona who, like her mother, was easily bored, and by the end of the week decided that if she were no further forward by the next weekend she would abandon her quest and go home.

Then on the Monday afternoon when she was sitting on the terrace with a book while both Leonie and Fiona were taking a siesta Blake Wantage walked across the garden and said: 'I've been making enquiries about your brother as I promised, and I think I've traced him.'

Marisa jumped to her feet, crying eagerly: 'Is he still here?'

'No.' Blake Wantage hesitated, then said uncompromisingly: 'Look, there's no easy way of breaking this, but

I'm very much afraid he's dead.'

'Dead?' Marisa stared at him incredulously. 'But—but he can't be!'

'A recruit named Michael William Farnham arrived here from Marseilles a year ago and was killed in a brawl five months later. It would be too much of a coincidence if it weren't your brother.'

'But this man couldn't have been Michael if he were killed in a brawl. Michael wouldn't fight anyone, he wasn't the violent type. Who told you all this?'

'Dr. Monet whom I know quite well introduced me to the commandant of the fort, who had the records searched for me. The personal effects of the man who was killed are still in the fort. If you could bear to examine them it would prove matters conclusively one way or the other.'

Marisa shivered, then braced herself. 'Anything's better than suspense. When can I see them?'

'We'll go now if you like.'

It was a silent drive into Calvi, and Marisa found it difficult to breathe as they parked the car before walking up to the Citadel. The pathetic bundle of possessions was produced and she clenched her teeth as she recognised the silver pencil she had given Michael for his eighteenth birthday and his watch. She dropped both into her handbag as the commandant expressed his regret, explaining that it had never been established exactly what had happened that night. All that was known was that there was a brawl in a bar, and when the military police arrived they found Michael lying unconscious under a table. He had a fractured skull, and had died without regaining consciousness.

Marisa thanked him and accompanied Blake Wantage back to the car without realising what she was doing. She felt completely numb, and quite unable to grasp that she would never see Michael again.

They were half way back to the villa when the car swerved to avoid a pothole and Marisa was jerked sideways, cracking her elbow against the door handle. It was

33

as if the sharp pain released something inside her, for without warning tears began to pour down her face. Blake Wantage said nothing, but pulled in to the side of the road and sat there until the storm of grief was spent.

At last she fumbled in her bag for a tissue, and muttered huskily: 'I'm sorry, I didn't mean to give way like that.'

He said remotely: 'You'll feel better now. As soon as we reach the villa you can take some aspirin with a cup of tea and lie down.'

'I still can't understand how it could have happened,' said Marisa hopelessly. 'Michael was impulsive sometimes, but he didn't drink much and I can't imagine him ever losing his temper sufficiently to hit a man.'

'It's a tough life in the Legion, and it could have altered him considerably.'

'I suppose so. What a dreadful waste! Michael had all his life before him.'

When they reached the villa Marisa fled to her room. She felt she must be by herself for a while, so when a knock came on her door she was tempted to pretend to be asleep, but in the end called: 'Come in!'

Blake Wantage entered with a tray of tea and a glass which he placed on the bedside table, saying: 'Take this aspirin, drink the tea and try to fall asleep.'

'But I ought to be looking after Fiona.'

'Never mind about Fiona. She'll be all right.'

Marisa swallowed the aspirin, then the tea, and lay down on her bed, determined to rest for just half an hour before going downstairs. However, to her surprise she dozed off, and when she awoke it was almost time for dinner. The sharp pangs of grief had numbed to a dull ache, so she forced herself to sponge her face and change into a dress. When she went downstairs Leonie was in the sitting-room, and her face told Marisa that she knew about Michael's death.

She said sympathetically: 'Let me pour you a glass of sherry,' and added: 'I was very sorry to hear about your brother. What will you do now?'

'There's no point in my staying here any longer. I'll ring the airport tomorrow and arrange a flight home.'

'Do you have to go home? I mean, have you anything special to do?'

'No, the house is shut up, but now I'll need to make plans and find a job.'

'Why don't you give yourself a break?' suggested Leonie, 'and spend the summer out here.'

'You mean you want me to continue to live here and look after Fiona?'

'Well, why not? The sun and sea air would do you good. Blake—' Leonie appealed to her brother-in-law who was just entering the room—'don't you think Miss Farnham ought to stay on here instead of rushing back to England?'

'That's for her to decide.'

'Yes, but—oh, well, think it over, Miss Farnham, and let me know in the morning.'

Marisa had plenty of time in which to make up her mind since she didn't fall asleep until after midnight. At first she was tempted to reject the offer right away. She was under no illusion as to Leonie's motives—the other woman was really only concerned to find someone willing to look after her child—but then she reflected that it would be very pleasant to spend the summer by the sea, and the task of keeping Fiona amused wasn't exactly arduous. Leonie, though frankly selfish and lazy, was easygoing and she would see so little of Blake Wantage that she hardly needed to consider him. He was a curious mixture, impatient and intolerant, yet he had taken the trouble to enquire about Michael for her and to bring her that tray of tea. It was impossible to weigh him up; the best thing would be to ignore him as much as possible. She turned over, suddenly decided to stay on at the villa, and slept.

When she woke the next morning she was still of the same mind, so seeing no point in dithering she announced her intention over breakfast on the terrace.

'Oh, good,' exclaimed Leonie. 'Let's start off on a more friendly basis and revert to Christian names. Do you agree, Blake?'

'Certainly, if it will make you feel happier,' he answered ironically. 'I'll be working all morning; ask Marie to bring me a tray for lunch, will you, please?'

Leonie grimaced as he disappeared. 'It's going to be uphill work for Giselle if she has ambitions to make Blake socially-minded. Still, if anyone can do it she can. She has everything—looks, money and personality.'

'She sounds rather overwhelming.'

'She gives most women an inferiority complex,' agreed Leonie. 'I can't understand why she isn't already married; she must have had dozens of opportunities.'

'But if she's waiting for your brother-in-law—?'

'I can only assume that she must be, though I wouldn't really have thought he was her type. However, that's their affair. I'm taking the car into Calvi this morning to have my hair done and I shall stay there for lunch. See you at dinner tonight.'

Marisa and Fiona spent the morning plunging in and out of the pool, and then while the little girl played with her dolls Marisa stretched out in a long chair on the terrace to consider her future. Should she take a job in London and continue to live in Clapham or should she sell the house and strike out somewhere fresh? She had never cared for town life very much and now that she had no one but herself to consider she could go where she pleased. The trouble was that she had no idea where she wanted to settle. A cottage in the country would be ideal, but would she be able to find work in its vicinity? Her uncle's stroke having forced her to leave school and run the house for him, she had had no chance to acquire any office experience.

She had still not made up her mind what to do by the time Leonie returned in the late afternoon. Roger was with her, and when Leonie announced that she intended to change into a bikini he came over to Marisa who was sitting by the pool with Fiona. He made sure that the little girl was busily occupied with a doll's tea-set and then turned sympathetically to Marisa.

'You'll guess, of course, that Leonie told me about your brother. There's not much I can say except that I'm sorry.'

'Thank you,' answered Marisa steadily.

'As it happened I'd heard something about that brawl in a bar, but I never connected it with him.'

'Did you learn any details?' asked Marisa eagerly. 'The commandant was very kind, but there was so little he could tell me.'

'I might be able to learn something more,' said Roger evasively. 'No promises, but I'll do my best.'

Leonie came back at that moment so no more was said, and after dinner she and Roger went to Calvi to visit a night spot. A couple of days later the telephone rang just before lunch, and Marie came out to announce disapprovingly that it was for Miss Farnham.

Leonie's eyes narrowed interrogatively as Marisa came back to the terrace.

'Was that Roger ringing you?' she enquired. 'It must have been; you don't know anyone else on the island.'

Marisa flushed. 'Yes, it was Roger. He asked me if I could meet him in Calvi this afternoon. He has some information for me about Michael.'

'Why couldn't he give it to you over the telephone?'

'He said he'd prefer to see me.'

'Would he indeed! Well, I don't think it will be convenient for you to have this afternoon off.'

Blake came up just in time to hear the last sentence, and he glanced from Marisa's flushed face to his sister-in-law's frown.

'What's all this?'

'Roger Dacre rang me a little while ago to say that he has something to tell me about Michael. He wants me to meet him in Calvi this afternoon.'

'So?'

Marisa looked at Leonie, who replied crossly: 'I'm going out myself this afternoon.'

'Then for once you can take Fiona with you,' retorted Blake crisply. 'Don't be ridiculous, Leonie. The salary you pay Marisa doesn't entitle you to keep her chained to the villa every hour of the day. Certainly she can go into Calvi this afternoon.'

Now it was Leonie's turn to flush, and her mouth tightened with temper.

'Who are you to dictate to me, Blake? You're not even my husband, only my brother-in-law.'

'Nevertheless this villa was lent to me, and if you want to continue staying here you'll have to behave in a reasonable fashion. As far as I'm concerned you can return to England any time you like.'

His face was implacable and Leonie bit her lip, then with an obvious effort climbed down.

'Take the afternoon off, Marisa, though you must admit it's rather short notice. I'll cope with Fiona.'

'Thank you,' murmured Marisa, feeling acutely embarrassed.

This wasn't going to improve the relationship between herself and Leonie, but she was too anxious to hear what Roger had to say to give way herself. She wanted to thank Blake for his intervention, but she could hardly do so in front of his sister-in-law, and anyway he was looking thoroughly bored with the whole business. She supposed that his sense of justice had prompted him to take her part. It certainly wasn't from any bias in her favour.

She had arranged to meet Roger by the Citadel since his car was under repair, and as she had no means of transport she was committed to walking the four miles into the town. Any other time she might have asked if she could borrow a car, but in this situation she had no intention of begging another favour, so she slipped away after lunch and put on a pair of crêpe-soled shoes. She was walking down the drive when a voice hailed her and warily she turned round.

'Where are you going?' demanded Blake as he approached her.

'To Calvi, of course,' answered Marisa.

'On foot?'

'It isn't really far, and I'm used to walking,' declared Marisa.

'Not in this heat,' pointed out Blake.

'It's not so very hot,' persisted Marisa mendaciously, and his mouth twitched.

'Don't be a little idiot! Swallow your pride and let me run you in.'

'I don't want to trouble you when I know you're busy.'

'I can be there and back in half an hour, though I'm surprised Dacre didn't come for you.'

'His car is in dock.'

'Then when he's told you all you want to know give me a ring and I'll come out for you.'

She opened her mouth to protest, then thought better of it and subsided meekly. In a very short time they had reached the Citadel and she saw Roger standing by the side of the road.

'Here you are,' said Blake curtly, 'and remember to ring me when you're ready to come home.'

He shot off as Roger approached, and the other man said: 'You were honoured if Wantage brought you into town. I thought Leonie would have lent you her car.'

'She was rather put out at my taking the afternoon off,' said Marisa ruefully. 'It wasn't very convenient for her.'

'Well, you can make it up to her another time,' said Roger carelessly. 'I thought you'd want to know as soon as possible what I'd found out, but I couldn't relate it all over the phone. Actually there's someone I think you should meet.'

'Someone who knew Michael?' cried Marisa.

'More than that—someone who was very close to him.'
Roger hesitated for a moment, then went on: 'I hope this

won't be too much of a shock for you, but it's a girl, and she says that your brother asked her to marry him.'

CHAPTER III

'Marry him?' gasped Marisa. 'Who is she? Where is she?'

'Steady on, let's sit down on this seat for a few minutes while I fill you in. Her name's Desirée Roland and she works in a bar-restaurant in one of the streets back from the sea-front.'

'How did you come across her?'

'Well, I asked around as I promised you I would, but I couldn't discover anyone who'd heard of your brother until Leonie happened to mention that he'd been identified as the legionnaire who'd been killed in a bar fight some months ago. When I knew that I tackled one of my acquaintances again who said he remembered the incident and that my best plan was to have a word with the proprietor of the bar, so I went along there.'

'And he told you about the girl?'

'No, he was reluctant to talk about the affair at all, so seeing I wasn't going to get anything out of him I turned away, and then this girl came after me. She asked me why I was enquiring about this legionnaire and I had to give her a reason, so I told her the truth, that his sister from England was here to find out what she could about his death. Then she said that she'd known him well, very well, and that he'd asked her to marry him.'

'Did you believe her?'

Roger gestured helplessly. 'I don't know, but she said she had proof. That's why I thought you ought to see her.'

'Oh yes, I must see her. Can we go to this bar now?'

'Of course. It's not far from the market.'

They left the Citadel, climbed a cobbled street behind the sea-front and near the colonnaded market came to a tiny courtyard with tubs of petunias and several small café tables. A swarthy black-browed man stood in the doorway of the bar itself, regarding them expressionlessly as they sat down, then he disappeared as a girl came forward to take their order. She was short with a ripe figure, a sulky mouth and large brown eyes, while her hair flowed down her back in a blue-black mass. She wasn't the type Marisa would have expected to appeal to Michael, but then the two years since he had left home could have changed him considerably.

Roger said: 'Marisa, this is Desirée Roland; Mademoiselle Roland, this is Mademoiselle Farnham.'

The girl stared at Marisa and said in stumbling, heavily accented English: 'You are the sister of Michel?'

Marisa answered: 'I think so, that is, if it was my brother you knew.'

'I knew Michel ver' well; he was my fiancé. You come *chez moi* I show you photograph and letters.'

'When?' asked Marisa.

The girl shrugged. 'Now if you wish. *Le patron* will give me leave for one hour.'

Marisa rose to her feet. 'Then don't let's lose any time.'

Roger looked dubious. 'Are you sure you want to go?' he asked. 'I could probably persuade her to bring the stuff here if she really has got it.'

'No, I want to see it now, not wait in suspense. Tell her I'm ready.'

The girl disappeared and returned in a moment wearing a cotton jacket over her black dress. She led the way to a narrow street at the back of the town where the stucco was peeling from the houses and the paint flaking from the shutters. She stopped to open a door with her key, and they followed her down a dark passage which led to a stuffy kitchen smelling strongly of garlic and olive oil. A fat, shapeless woman was lifting a coffee pot from the

41

stove and a man, unshaven and collarless, sat in a wooden armchair puffing at a cheroot.

Obviously these were the girl's parents and they stared suspiciously at Marisa and Roger. Desirée in a burst of rapid French explained who the visitors were and left them standing there uncomfortably, while Madame Roland replaced the coffee pot on the stove and lowered herself on to a stool. In a few moments Desirée returned with a box which she opened, and taking a snapshot from it she thrust it at Marisa. It showed Desirée in a bikini sitting on the beach with a man whose arm was round her shoulders, and Marisa swallowed hard. The man was definitely Michael.

Wordlessly she held the photo out to Roger, who looked at it and then said interrogatively: 'This is your brother?'

Marisa nodded. 'Yes, that's Michael. There's no doubt of it.'

Desirée plunged into the box again, and this time she brought out a letter and a ring set with two small diamonds and a ruby.

Indicating the ring, she said: 'Michel, he give me for our betrothal,' and then held out the letter. It was written in French, but the handwriting was unmistakably Michael's, and Marisa could make out enough of it to be sure that it was a love letter. There didn't seem any reason to disbelieve Desirée when she declared that he had asked her to marry him.

Marisa said helplessly: 'It looks as though she's telling the truth, but how can I be sure?'

'You can't,' answered Roger, and turned to Desirée, speaking in French.

'You say that Michael asked you to marry him, but how would that be possible? He had almost fifteen years to serve in the Legion and was due to be posted away from Corsica very soon.'

'He had a plan to desert and when he arrived in England he was to send for me. He told me his uncle had much money and he promised me money to support my parents. They are infirm and cannot work; they depend upon me.'

Madame Roland, gazing first at one face, then another, said something to her daughter which Marisa couldn't catch. The girl hissed a reply, then said to Marisa: 'Michel, he promised me money many times. Your uncle, he will send it now?'

'My uncle died a short while ago,' Marisa told her, and then became aware that her head was throbbing madly and that if she didn't get out of this stifling atmosphere she would be sick.

She said urgently to Roger: 'Let's go, I can't stand it in here any longer,' and made for the door.

Desirée rushed after her and grabbed her arm.

'I have more letters from your brother; you wish to read them?'

'Not now,' said Marisa. 'I will see you again at the restaurant,' and emerging into the fresh air she moved thankfully away from the house, leaving Desirée standing sulkily in the doorway.

'How could Michael have wanted to marry her?' she burst out as she and Roger walked down the cobbled street together. 'She's so far removed from the type of girl he professed to admire.'

'Perhaps his taste had altered,' suggested Roger dryly. 'Little brothers have a habit of growing up, you know, and Desirée's got a lot of sex appeal.'

Marisa flushed. 'I suppose she has, but that Michael, of all people—however, it's no use dwelling on that. The question is, what do I do about her?'

'Desirée? Nothing at all, I should think.'

'It's not quite as simple as that. If Michael were going to marry her and he did promise her money for her parents there's a certain obligation on me to carry out his wishes.'

Roger stared at her. 'You must be crazy! Michael's dead and that's the end of the matter as far as she's con-

43

cerned. Your best plan is to go back to England and forget all about her.'

'I can't do that. I'll have to think matters out.'

'Well, in the meantime come and have a drink, then what about walking to the beach for a swim?'

'No, I must go back to the villa. I'll ring Blake and tell him I'm ready.'

'If only my car wasn't laid up I could take you myself. I wish now I'd never told you about Desirée Roland. It would have been far better for you not to have learned about her.'

'No, I'd rather have known. At least she may have made life a little happier for Michael while he was here.'

They walked into a nearby bar where Marisa rang the villa and left a message for Blake. While they waited for him Roger ordered drinks and Marisa said: 'Shall you stay here all winter or go back to England?'

'I'm not sure. I don't think I could settle down to a nine-to-five job after this bout of freedom.'

'But you can't go on drifting for ever.'

He sighed in mock sorrow. 'The trouble with women is that they always want to reform you; they're never satisfied with you as you are. Just because Wantage is a worthy type and keeps his nose to the grindstone we don't all have to follow his example.'

'I never suggested you should,' said Marisa indignantly. 'And Blake isn't a worthy type. I mean—oh, I don't know what I mean,' she finished crossly.

Roger grinned. 'Girls as pretty as you don't need to mean anything.'

'Save your compliments for Leonie,' answered Marisa severely.

'Don't you appreciate them?' murmured Roger, and then his tone altered. 'Ah, here's your chauffeur,' and impudently he leaned across the table to kiss Marisa full on the mouth just as Blake's car drew to a halt on the opposite side of the road.

Marisa jumped to her feet in some confusion, but it

was impossible to tell from Blake's impassive expression as he crossed towards them whether he had seen the incident or not.

'Ready?' he enquired as he reached Marisa, and hastily she replied: 'Yes, quite.'

'I'll be off,' said Roger casually. 'Goodbye, my sweet, I'll see you soon,' and he sauntered away.

Blake said nothing at all, and annoyed as she was with Roger for his behaviour Marisa deemed it wiser not to embark on any explanations herself. As he opened the car door for her Blake asked: 'Have you learned anything more about your brother? Has Dacre been able to throw any light on the incident which led to his death?'

'No, nothing like that. What he wanted to tell me was that he'd contacted a girl who'd known Michael while he was here. Roger took me to meet her in the bar-restaurant near the market where she works. She told me that she was engaged to Michael, that he planned to desert from the Legion and get back to England, then send for her.'

'Had she any proof of this?' enquired Blake.

'Yes. She took us to her home where she showed me a ring which she said Michael had given her, also a photo and a letter. The photograph was of herself and Michael on the beach with his arm round her. The letter was a love letter. I couldn't translate every word of it, but it was in Michael's handwriting and I understood enough to know that he must have been in love with her.'

'Hard luck on the pair of them that it had to end so tragically, though I don't think your brother would have found it easy to desert from the Legion. Not many people have managed it.'

'No, I suppose not. Poor Michael, he never had much happiness. He didn't get on with my uncle, and then when he made his bid for freedom it was to a life equally hard.'

'It was rather a dramatic gesture to make, wasn't it?' commented Blake dryly. 'Surely he could have asserted his individuality without going to such lengths? Did he never consider you?'

45

'But why should he consider me?' exclaimed Marisa in astonishment. 'It was never as bad for me as it was for him, partly because I was younger when our parents died and partly because I got on better with Uncle William.'

Blake arched one eyebrow sceptically, and Marisa felt her temper rise, though she managed to choke it down. Why did she always seem to be at cross purposes with Blake and long to ruffle his composure?

Then she sighed inwardly. It was stupid to allow trifles to bother her when she had a far more serious problem to solve. Desirée Roland was the real crux of the matter. Was there a moral obligation to do something for her because it was what Michael would have wished?

With her mind in a turmoil Marisa gave herself up to her thoughts, and was startled when Blake said suddenly: 'What's worrying you now?'

She stammered: 'Nothing,' aware that she didn't sound in the least convincing and met his cool, appraising stare with a defiantly lifted chin.

'You're a very poor liar,' he remarked conversationally. 'Anyone could see that something's troubling you. Is this girl pregnant?'

Marisa blinked. 'No, I'm sure she isn't, otherwise she would have mentioned it, because—'

She stopped short, and he prompted: 'Because——?'

'She told me that Michael had promised to help her parents financially, and if she had been expecting his child she must have known that it would strengthen her case.'

'Her case? Do you mean she's asked you for money?'

'Yes.'

Marisa braced herself for his scorn, but he said nothing at all until the car was turning in at the gates to the villa. Then he advised with surprising mildness: 'Go back to England, Marisa, and forget that you ever came to Corsica. You're out of your depth in this set-up.'

It was obvious that he didn't think much of her intelligence, and with a queer sense of hurt she protested: 'I

46

can't just close my eyes and ignore facts. When Uncle William died he left the house and what money there was to me, but I intended to share it with Michael as soon as I could trace him. Now I'm wondering if I ought to hand over his share to Desirée Roland, whether that's what he would have wished.'

She stared defiantly at Blake, who stared back with an unfathomable expression. Then he slid out of the car and came round to open the door for Marisa.

'Why don't you remain passive for the moment?' he suggested. 'Do nothing at all, but go on staying here for the rest of the summer and see what develops.'

Relief surged over the girl. Blake was right. There was no need for her to come to a decision right away; she could afford to postpone it. She could get to know Desirée Roland better, and then make up her mind what Michael would have wanted her to do.

She said hesitatingly: 'You don't think that would be cowardly? I mean, just putting things off—?'

He answered gravely: 'No, I don't. I think it would be sensible to consider things carefully before acting.'

They walked into the villa together, and before they parted Marisa attempted to express her gratitude.

'Thank you for helping me today—in every way.'

He said curtly: 'Not at all,' and immediately went out to the studio. Going in search of Leonie Marisa thought for the hundredth time what an unpredictable man he was—reacting with sympathy when she had expected derision and then immediately sheering off from her. She was sure she would never understand him.

Leonie received the information about Desirée Roland coolly, but she had a letter at breakfast the next morning which diverted her mind from everything else.

'Giselle's coming over at the weekend,' she exclaimed. 'Originally she intended to wait until her father could get away as well, but now she says that London's so stuffy she's longing for some sea air. Have you had a letter from her too, Blake?' noticing that there was a thick cream

47

envelope by his plate.

'Yes. She says much the same thing to me.'

'But at greater length, I'm sure,' commented Leonie slyly. 'I must tell Marie.'

But Marie was able to announce triumphantly that she already knew, that she also had received a letter. She demanded that Jean should drive her into Calvi to shop since there were special things Mademoiselle Giselle would require, and the whole villa was thrown into bustle and confusion.

There were six bedrooms in the villa, the one usually reserved for Giselle being occupied at the moment by Leonie.

'Now I must move into the room next to you,' she sighed to Marisa, 'and when Giselle's father arrives you'll have to share with Fiona. I hate leaving this bedroom with all its space for my clothes and the balcony looking out over the garden. I can't think why Giselle should want to advance her holiday—or rather I can. I expect Marie's written to her and told her about you.'

'But what difference could I make to her plans?' queried Marisa in surprise.

'Where Giselle's concerned you're a potential rival. I told you she regarded Blake as her property.'

'But that's ridiculous! I'm sure he never gives me a second thought.'

Leonie said: 'That may be so, but Giselle won't take any chances.' Then she brightened. 'But there's one thing to the good, we'll probably be caught up in a social whirl. If I know Giselle she won't be content to stay in every evening.'

After that outpouring Leonie said no more, but rested after lunch, then disappeared in her car leaving Marisa with Fiona. They had their usual session in the pool where Fiona had now lost all fear of the water and could triumphantly swim a few strokes, then the little girl said fretfully: 'What can I do now?'

'We could have a doll's tea-party,' suggested Marisa,

48

pulling forward the two charmingly dressed dolls and the teddy bear which were lying at the edge of the pool. 'Shall we go and fetch the tea-set and some milk and biscuits?'

'No,' declared Fiona crossly. 'Don't want to play with stupid dolls and a stupid teddy. I'm tired of them!' and she kicked out with her bare foot to push them over again.

Marisa sympathised with her. It was very boring for the child with no one of her own age to play with. She had a quantity of expensive toys but nothing on which to use her imagination. At four years old she needed the rough and tumble of family life with brothers and sisters or the stimulation of play-school, but when Marisa had hinted this to her mother Leonie had said carelessly: 'Oh, I think you're exaggerating.'

'I'm sure she misses her friends at home,' insisted Marisa. 'Isn't there anyone near by with whom she could play?'

'Most of the villas are let to holiday people who only stay for a fortnight or so, and I'm certainly not calling on them to invite them up here even if they could all speak English, which isn't very likely. You'll just have to manage as best you can. After all, Fiona has the pool and all the garden to play in.'

So Marisa racked her brains to devise ways of amusing her charge, and had observed that Fiona had a distinct talent for drawing. Unfortunately there were no materials in the villa to foster this. She had a small colouring book and some crayons, but no paints or chalks, not even a large sheet of paper. It occurred to Marisa that Blake might be able to help in this respect, and knowing that he was working in the studio she decided to tackle him this afternoon.

Marie usually took him a tray of tea about four o'clock, so Marisa said: 'Perhaps Uncle Blake could let you have a big sheet of paper to draw on. We'll take his pot of tea across to him and ask him.'

'Oh, yes.' Fiona brightened immediately. 'I'li make a
49

picture, a big picture. I'll draw the pantomime I saw at Christmas, shall I?'

'That would be a good idea,' agreed Marisa. 'Come along, we'll go to the kitchen.'

Fiona skipped along in her brief yellow swimsuit, chattering excitedly, while Marisa prayed that Blake would be in an amiable mood. She collected the tray of tea from Marie and carried it across to the studio where Fiona had the door open before Marisa could even knock.

'Uncle Blake, Uncle Blake!' cried the little girl 'We've come for a piece of paper, a big piece so I can draw my picture.'

'I thought you might have some,' said Marisa apologetically, laying down the tray. 'I suppose you haven't any paints or chalks Fiona could use?' she added hopefully.

'Hardly,' he answered. 'Why this sudden artistic urge?'

'She gets so bored just playing with dolls,' Marisa explained. 'She needs something to occupy her mind and she's really quite clever at drawing; didn't you know?'

'No, but then I haven't really seen a great deal of Fiona. This is the first time we've spent more than the odd half hour together.'

'But I thought you and your brother lived fairly close to each other?'

'Not far apart,' conceded Blake, but since he was obviously not going to enlarge on that Marisa said no more on the subject, though she couldn't help wondering if he and his brother hadn't much in common why Blake had invited Leonie and Fiona to spend the summer with him in the villa. Now she urged: 'You do have some paper?'

'That I can supply, but surely it isn't much use if Fiona hasn't anything to draw with?'

'She has some coloured pencils.'

'They're scarcely ideal. Suppose we go into Calvi and see what the town can supply?'

'Oh, I don't want to interrupt your work,' protested

Marisa.

'I've more or less finished for the day. Get some clothse on and I'll be ready in a quarter of an hour.'

For the first time Marisa became conscious that she was wearing only a bikini. Since Blake had seen her in this scanty attire many times already it needn't have troubled her, but all at once she felt embarrassed. A burning tide of colour swept over her face and she grabbed Fiona's arm.

'Come along,' she said hastily, 'we'll have to hurry so as not to keep Uncle Blake waiting.'

In ten minutes she had changed into cotton slacks and shirt, and pushed Fiona into shorts and a tee-shirt. Then they ran through the hall and out on to the gravel drive where Blake had already brought the car round.

'Punctual too,' he commented. 'You have all the virtues.'

Marisa looked at him warily. 'Look, you don't have to drive us into Calvi. I didn't expect you to when I asked for the paper.'

He opened the rear door of the car for Fiona to scramble in.

'What makes you think I don't want to drive you into Calvi?'

'When you're sarcastic it's usually a sign that you're put out,' responded Marisa frankly.

'I'd no idea you'd made such a study of my character,' he said solemnly, then he grinned. 'For once I wasn't being sarcastic, so hop in and let's get going.'

Marisa's spirits rose with a bound, though she couldn't have said exactly why. After all, why should she feel so happy at the prospect of driving into Calvi with Blake and Fiona; surely it was a very commonplace outing.

But the fact remained that at that moment she would have wished herself nowhere else. Blake found a stationer's shop where they were able to buy large sheets of paper, a big drawing book, thick chalks and some tubes of paint and brushes. Marisa, prowling round the shop while he

51

made his selection, came across a child's alphabet book, surprisingly enough in English, and bought it. At four Fiona wasn't too young to start learning her letters and it might help to occupy her when she was tired of drawing.

When they had finished in the stationer's they came out into the sunlight again, and Fiona remarked hopefully: 'I'm thirsty.'

Her uncle looked down at her. 'So am I. What about a *sirop* at that café over there?'

They sat down under an awning, and Fiona had a long fizzy drink while Marisa and Blake drank vermouth and soda. As they sat there pleasantly relaxed Marisa began to ask him about his work, and he mentioned the assignment which was currently occupying him.

'It's very much of a prestige project,' he told her, 'and it would be extremely helpful to us in the future if we could win this contract. As you can imagine in the present economic climate there's a great deal of competition for any commissions which are in the offing, so it's a question of combining originality and practicality, which isn't easy.'

'I can understand that,' agreed Marisa.

'One of the difficulties is to fit everything in without building too high; it's also necessary to make as much use as possible of local materials to cut transport costs.'

He had the knack of painting a vivid picture in a few words, and as he talked Marisa found she could visualise the shopping precinct he described with its different levels all centred round the old Regency theatre which had been rescued from demolition.

'It all sounds really exciting,' she remarked, and Blake answered: 'To me it is, but I'm afraid I must have been boring you.'

'You weren't in the least,' denied Marisa, and he said consideringly: 'You should have been an architect yourself.'

'I should have liked a career,' confessed Marisa, 'and I stayed on at school to study for A-levels, but just as I'd taken them Uncle William had his first stroke, which meant my leaving school to look after him and run the house.'

'Well, housekeeping can be an art in itself. Giselle Lambert oversees her father's house very successfully and does a good deal of entertaining for him.'

'Uncle William wasn't very fond of visitors,' said Marisa wryly. 'He had an old friend who used to play chess with him sometimes and stay to supper, but that was all.'

'And what about your friends?'

'Well, as I said, my uncle didn't encourage visitors, so I rather lost touch with most of my school friends, but I wasn't unhappy because I could fill any spare time with reading.'

Once again Blake gave her an unfathomable look, then said: 'We'd better be moving,' so the three of them walked back to the car.

For the rest of the week Marisa saw very little of him, and she wondered if he were working particularly hard so that he could be free when Giselle Lambert arrived. On the Saturday he went off to the airport to meet her, and Marisa found herself holding her breath when they heard the car returning.

She lingered in the background, and presently heard a light voice reply to Leonie's enquiry about the journey with: 'Oh, it was so boring on the plane. I had a fat little Frenchman next to me who snored all the way, but when I came through the Customs at Bastia to find Blake waiting for me the day began to improve at once.'

'I'm flattered,' returned Blake, and the next moment Giselle appeared.

Marisa's first thought was that she was even more attractive than reports had suggested. Her hair, presumably a legacy from her French mother, was glossily dark, and her almond-shaped eyes were a tawny gold, set off by her creamy skin. She wasn't tall, but she was beautifully proportioned, and her figure was enhanced by a perfectly cut trouser suit in an uncrushable cream fabric.

She cast a cursory glance at Marisa, and then as Leonie introduced them the newcomer's lips widened into a smile which didn't reach her eyes as she said: 'I hope you're enjoying your summer in the sun.'

'Very much,' answered Marisa politely, realising instinctively that she had been summed up and dismissed as negligible.

'I must have a bath,' announced Giselle. 'I feel so sticky after the journey. Come and talk to me, Leonie, and tell me all the news.'

The two of them disappeared and as Blake also vanished Marisa was left alone with Fiona. The little girl pushed out her bottom lip and said: 'Don't like that lady.'

Marisa agreed with her entirely, but thought it best to ignore the observation.

'Let's go for a swim,' she suggested. 'See if you can race me across the pool.'

Fiona agreed enthusiastically, and the two of them were soon disporting themselves. It wasn't until a voice said indulgently: 'How very competent you are, Miss Farnham,' that Marisa realised Giselle was walking towards the pool. She blinked the water out of her eyes to see the other girl drop gracefully down on to the scarlet canvas lounger which showed up her white swimsuit to maximum advantage.

Giselle contrived to make it sound more of an insult than a compliment, and Marisa gritted her teeth. She dived to swim underwater, and managed to inveigle Fiona to the far end of the pool. Before long, however, the little girl wanted to scramble out, so Marisa was obliged to emerge herself and to saunter over to where Giselle and Leonie were sunbathing since Fiona had chosen to lean against her mother's feet.

'What happened to Sue?' enquired Giselle lazily. 'I thought she was to help with Fiona.'

'She and Martin patched up things at the last moment.

Now she's working in a boutique and living in a flat above it.'

'And how's Jon?'

Leonie grimaced. 'Wedded to his work, as usual.'

'Isn't he coming out here to join you?'

'Yes, later on. He's always so reluctant to take holidays. He's afraid the bank will collapse without him.'

'You're not afraid he might seek distraction elsewhere while you're away?'

Leonie snapped: 'No, I'm not.'

'Well, you ought to know,' murmured Giselle. 'Personally I don't believe in exposing any man to temptation.'

'Is that why you've decided to come out here earlier than you first planned?'

'There's no harm in taking every precaution,' declared Giselle, quite unruffled. 'Fiona darling, wouldn't you like to come and sit on the end of my chair?'

'No,' retorted Fiona uncompromisingly.

'No, thank you,' said Blake sternly, appearing round the thicket of bushes which sheltered one side of the pool. 'Where are your manners?'

Marisa felt absurdly guilty as if she were responsible for Fiona's ungraciousness. She wanted to get away from Giselle's coldly appraising eyes, so she held out a hand to Fiona, saying: 'Come along, we'll go for a walk and see if we can find some wild flowers.'

But Fiona was in a contrary mood and shook her head. 'Want to stay with Mummy.'

'I'm afraid we're neither of us in favour today, Miss Farnham,' remarked Giselle sweetly. 'Blake, I'm longing to go round to the Bay for a lobster lunch. When will you take me?'

'Where's the Bay?' enquired Leonie.

'A few miles along the coast. There's a beach bar at the far end not much more than a shack, but they specialise in serving lobster. I've been there many times, and last year I introduced Blake to it.'

'It sounds attractive, and I adore lobster.'

55

'Then the three of us will go. It wouldn't be much fun for Fiona. She'll be far better staying here at the pool with Miss Farnham.'

That puts me nicely in my place, thought Marisa wryly. She was aware that Leonie was looking slightly uncomfortable, but it was Blake who said: 'Oh, I think Fiona might enjoy it too, not the lobster but the bathing at the Bay. We'll all go.'

For a second Giselle's lips were compressed into a hard, thin line, but in a moment she was smiling again.

'Then it's settled. Shall we say Monday? By the way, Blake, I've arranged to hire a car so that I can run myself about. I want to collect it this evening, so will you run me into Calvi?'

'Yes, of course.'

Giselle's arrival made quite a difference to the routine of the household, Marie emphasising her position as the owner's daughter by providing much more elaborate meals. Giselle herself was careful to see that Blake's wishes were respected and consulted Leonie frequently, but Marisa she more or less ignored and the girl was sure that if Giselle had dared she would have treated her as another servant.

The new arrival was absent from the villa most of the next day visiting friends, but she appeared at breakfast on the Monday morning in a very becoming lime green cotton trouser suit with a thin white ribbed cotton sweater to say: 'It's a perfect day for a trip to the Bay. What time shall we set off, Blake?'

'I thought about half-past ten,' he replied, 'then we shall have time for a bathe before lunch.'

'Yes, that's a good idea. We'd better take two cars. You and I can travel in mine and the others in Leonie's.'

Marisa had imagined they would all go in one car since there was plenty of room for three in the back of Blake's, but he made no protest and they set off in two separate parties. They drove through the town and continued along the coast road until it reached a sandy bay backed

56

by pines on which stood an open-fronted building which was the lobster restaurant. Inside were benches and rough wooden tables covered with coarse white cloths already set out with cutlery and carafes of wine.

At the back of the restaurant were two changing huts, one for men and one for women, and it wasn't long before they all emerged to plunge into the water. Marisa stayed with Fiona in the shallows while after the briefest of dips Leonie spread her towel on a convenient slab of rock and sunbathed. Giselle was a good swimmer and she and Blake had soon left the shore behind, so that it was a surprise to Marisa when he eventually turned and swam back towards her to say: 'Leave Fiona to me while you go off for a swim yourself.'

She needed no further urging, and was soon cleaving the water before eventually turning back for the shore again. When she reached it Blake was patiently instructing Fiona while Giselle looked on.

'Oh, here's Marisa at last,' she cried, and Marisa noted the use of her christian name, wondering if Blake had commented on Giselle's continual 'Miss Farnham'. 'Now we can go in for lunch.'

'I'm sorry if I've kept you all waiting,' apologised Marisa.

'You haven't,' declared Leonie lazily. 'We didn't set any definite time.'

Giselle slipped her arm through Blake's, and saying gaily: 'Lead on, Macduff, I'm ravenous!' urged him into the restaurant, the others following.

The lobster was certainly delicious and they all did justice to it, an omelette being provided for Fiona. They lingered to finish their wine until at last Leonie declared that she was so sleepy she could scarcely keep her eyes open.

'I shall go into the shade for a siesta,' she announced firmly, 'and take Fiona with me for her nap.'

'I hate dozing in the middle of the day,' said Giselle, 'and I know you do, Blake, so you can finish telling me about your Town Centre plans. Daddy's dying to know how they're coming on.'

Having no wish to play gooseberry Marisa said quickly: 'I think I'll go for a stroll along the beach,' and set off immediately.

She walked along until presently the sand was bisected by a long outcrop of rock culminating in a flat slab. Having decided to sit there for a few minutes Marisa gave a short leap to reach it, but her foot slipped, bringing her down on the rocks with a crash. Her forehead struck a sharp edge and for a second she was stunned, then she levered herself upright with the blood trickling down her face.

Feeling sick, she crawled shakily back along the rocks to the sand where she forced herself to stand up and walk jerkily back to the restaurant. If possible she wanted to avoid a fuss, so holding her handkerchief to the cut on her hair line she tried to appear as normal as possible.

Giselle and Blake were still sitting talking at the table as she approached, and he jumped up as soon as he saw her.

'What's the matter?' he enquired. 'Have you hurt yourself?'

'It's nothing much, just a graze. I slipped on the rocks.' Blake took her arm to steer her to a chair. 'Sit back,' he ordered, 'and don't move.'

He disappeared into the rear of the restaurant, and returned in a few moments with a first-aid box.

'That cut needs a stitch,' he observed. 'Come along, we'll get you to a doctor.'

'Really, there's no need for that,' Marisa protested.

'Is it absolutely necessary, Blake?' asked Giselle. 'I'm sure Marisa doesn't want a lot of fuss.'

He fixed a temporary dressing over the wound, then said: 'A gash like that needs professional attention if it isn't to leave a permanent scar.'

'Then I'll drive Marisa to the doctor. He's an old friend.'

It was the last thing Marisa wanted, and her relief was enormous when Blake said: 'No, I'll take her. You drive Leonie and Fiona back to the villa.'

It was obvious that this didn't suit Giselle at all, but she could hardly insist on having her own way. She shrugged her shoulders pettishly, and Marisa found herself in the car on the way to the doctor almost before she realised what was happening.

When it was all over and she was leaving his surgery, armed with a sedative together with instructions to lie down for the rest of the day and come to see him a week hence, she had time to reflect how amazingly gentle Blake could be. He settled her comfortably and competently in the car, and when she tried shakily to apologise for spoiling the day for all of them he said cheerfully: 'Don't worry about that. Let's be thankful you didn't break a leg.'

By the time the villa was reached Marisa's head was throbbing violently and all she wanted was to lie down in her cool bedroom. After one glance at her Blake had concentrated on his driving, and as he helped her out of the car he said: 'Would you like me to carry you, or can you walk?'

'I can walk,' gasped Marisa, but she was glad of his hand under her elbow and once inside the bedroom she sank down on the bed.

Blake bent to ease off her sandals, then swung her legs on to the bed and covered her with a light blanket.

'Lie still,' he ordered, 'and I'll ask Marie to help you undress.'

As soon as he had left her, however, Marisa struggled out of her clothes and managed to drag her nightdress over her head. When Marie at last appeared she was lying back with her eyes closed, and having asked for a glass of water so that she could swallow the tablets the doctor had given her intimated that she wanted to be left alone.

She must have dozed off almost immediately, because when she woke the pain in her head had subsided to a dull ache, and she no longer felt sick. She winced as her fingers touched the plaster on her forehead, then cautiously she sat up. Since she didn't feel faint or dizzy she ventured to stand, grimacing as she saw her pale face in the mirror opposite. It was an effort to wash and put on a dress, but she felt better afterwards and able to go downstairs.

To her surprise Blake was on the terrace, and he frowned when he saw her.

'Didn't the doctor tell you to stay in bed for the rest of the day?'

'I felt so much better that I preferred to come down.'

'Then you must lie back in this chair and not talk.'

He settled her competently before returning to the plans he was studying. Rather hazily she gazed at him and said: 'Why aren't you working in the studio as usual?'

'Because the others have gone into Calvi and I thought someone should remain within call in case you needed anything.'

She blinked. 'Fancy you thinking of that. It was nice of you.'

For a second there was a curious expression on his face, then it vanished.

'Go to sleep,' he said, and meekly she obeyed.

CHAPTER IV

In the morning her forehead was still tender, but otherwise she had nearly recovered. Leonie greeted her appearance at the breakfast table with relief, and Marisa suspected that she had been afraid she would be saddled with Fiona for the rest of the week. The little girl was in high spirits, and having conquered her fear of the water clamoured to be in and out of the pool.

Leonie shot a sidelong glance at Marisa, and Blake said firmly: 'You must play quietly in the garden this morning and I'll take you into the pool this afternoon.'

Fiona pouted. 'Want Marisa to swim with me now.'

'Perhaps if we just paddled in the shallow end,' suggested Marisa, but Blake vetoed that.

'No. You don't want to get that dressing wet.'

Giselle said: 'I'll take you into the pool darling,' and got up from the breakfast table on the terrace to go into the house.

Emerging in a flesh-coloured bikini which highlighted her superb figure and left absolutely nothing to the imagination, she stepped into the shallow end of the pool and Fiona scampered after her, splashing vigorously. Giselle, whose gleaming hair lay on her shoulders, protested laughingly, but frolicked with the child until Blake left the terrace, when her mood changed abruptly.

'That's enough,' she said, and picking Fiona up dumped her on the side of the pool before climbing out herself.

'But I want to swim!' cried Fiona.

'And I don't,' declared Giselle, stretching out on a canvas lounger. 'Play with your doll.'

Fiona's mouth drooped, but sensing instinctively that tears would avail her nothing she trotted into the villa in search of her mother or Marisa, who had both left the terrace just before Blake.

She found Marisa tidying her bedroom, and begged: 'Will you play with me? She won't swim now.'

Marisa, guessing the situation, suggested: 'Shall we read a book in the shade and later on you can have some lemonade?'

'Yes, please,' answered Fiona philosophically, and they went down into the garden together.

There was a white wrought-iron seat under the acacia tree together with a table on which Marisa spread the alphabet book. Fiona was taking a keen interest in

61

learning her letters and already knew most of them off by heart. The illustrations were charming, and Marisa had woven a little story about each of them which Fiona demanded to hear after she had named the correct letter. She had already opened the book when there was the sound of a car and in a few moments Roger appeared.

At the same time Leonie came on to the terrace and cried: 'Roger, where have you been all this time? I thought you must have gone back to England.'

'No, but since my car was repaired I've been to one or two places to collect material for an article I've been commissioned to do for a magazine. There's a new hotel opened just along the coast which I wondered if you and Marisa would like to sample for lunch today.' He grinned. 'Special terms to me for mentioning it in the article.'

His glance took in Giselle and his eyes widened in appreciation.

'I see you've got another visitor. Well, the more the merrier.'

Leonie introduced them, adding: 'Roger is a freelance journalist and teacher of English. He has a flat in the Citadel in Calvi.'

'The operative word is "free",' commented Roger boldly, and Giselle smiled entrancingly.

'Thank you for your invitation. I'm in the mood for experimenting.'

'Then what are we waiting for?' asked Roger. He looked across at Marisa. 'Hallo, poppet, what about it?'

'Thank you, Roger, but not today,' she answered.

He walked across the gravel and peered at her. 'What's the matter? How did you hurt your forehead?'

'I fell on the rocks yesterday. It was all my own fault and it's nothing serious, but I don't feel like lunching out.'

'Yes, it will be far better for you to rest in the garden,' declared Giselle with false sympathy. She turned to Roger. 'Give me ten minutes to put on some clothes.'

She sauntered into the villa and Roger said: 'Sorry you

can't come, Marisa, but there's ample time for a return visit.'

'I want to go with you,' cried Fiona, scrambling off the seat and running over to her mother.

'Not today, darling, some other time,' answered Leonie perfunctorily. 'You stay in the garden with Marisa.'

Roger looked slightly uncomfortable. 'Perhaps we ought to postpone the trip,' he began, but at that moment Giselle appeared looking ravishing in pale yellow, her dark hair tied back with a matching chiffon scarf. His doubts obviously vanished as he gazed at her with admiration, and she gave him no opportunity for further hesitation

'Forward,' she said gaily, and Roger, taking both her arm and Leonie's, swept them out to his car.

Marisa, left alone with Fiona, felt a pang of disappointment, but stifled it.

'Now we'll carry on with our lesson,' she told the little girl, who was inclined to be tearful, 'and then we'll have a picnic, just you, me and the dolls.'

It didn't take much to distract Fiona, and soon she was busy identifying the letters in the alphabet book, then listening to the stories Marisa wove about them. They were both so absorbed that they never heard Blake crossing the gravel in his espadrilles, and Marisa started when he said: 'I thought you were supposed to be resting. Where are Leonie and Giselle?'

Marisa hesitated, but Fiona piped up: 'They've gone out in the car with that man called Roger. I wanted to go too, but they wouldn't take me.'

Blake looked questioningly at Marisa, who said quickly: 'Roger came to invite us to sample a new hotel which has opened along the coast, but I didn't feel in the mood for it today.'

'So they left you to look after Fiona.'

'She's really no trouble, and you can't say I'm exerting myself by telling her a story.'

'What's the book?' Blake picked it up to study it.

'I hope you approve, but Fiona's very intelligent and she gets so bored playing all the time, so I've been teaching her her letters, trying to make it fun rather than work. I suppose I should have consulted her mother really, but I didn't think Leonie would mind.'

'Where did you buy this book?'

'In the shop where you bought the drawing materials.'

'Look, Uncle Blake, there's C for cat,' pointed out Fiona, 'and D for donkey too.'

He took her right through the alphabet, and found she could name almost all the letters.

'I know some people think that you shouldn't encourage a child to learn too early, but I haven't forced Fiona at all,' said Marisa.

'No, it's easy to see she's wanted to learn. It will be a good thing when she starts nursery school to bring her into contact with other children and change Leonie's way of life.'

He stopped short as if regretting having said so much and asked: 'Were there any other children's books in the shop?'

'I think so. I'd already decided to have another look the next time I'm in Calvi to see if there was something else suitable for Fiona.'

'We might try our luck tomorrow. I'll run you into Calvi in the morning.'

'I want to go into Calvi,' exclaimed Fiona automatically, but her uncle shook his head. 'No, not tomorrow, because Marisa and I have shopping to do.'

He rose to his feet, and Fiona said coaxingly: 'Play with me, Uncle Blake, play hide and seek.'

'I can't now because I have some work to do, but I'll play with you tomorrow.'

'Hide and seek?'

'Anything you choose.'

He went away and Fiona sighed, 'I wish I could go home to Daddy.'

It was the first time she had mentioned her father, and Marisa was intrigued.

She asked: 'Does your daddy look like Uncle Blake?'

Fiona said vaguely: 'He can swing me right up into the air, only he doesn't come home until I'm in bed because he has to work very hard. Mummy said I would see him soon, but he hasn't come yet and it's a very long time.'

'Perhaps he'll be here in a week or two,' said Marisa cautiously, not wishing to raise false hopes. 'Sit back and I'll finish the story about the family of squirrels who lived in the hollow tree.'

Marisa suspected that Blake had rounded on his sister-in-law for leaving Marisa with Fiona, because Leonie looked both defiant and guilty when they assembled for dinner that evening. She enthused over the hotel to which Roger had taken them, and said: 'We must make up a party for a return visit one evening. I'm sure you'd enjoy it, Blake.'

'It really is a delightful spot, Blake,' put in Giselle. 'You could invite Roger, Leonie, and perhaps he could ask another man as a partner for Marisa.'

'I'd be quite happy to stay at home with Fiona,' said Marisa.

'Nonsense, we wouldn't dream of it,' returned Giselle sweetly. 'You must come along too.'

'Or we could wait until your father arrives and then we'd be an even number,' suggested Leonie, and Giselle agreed immediately: 'Yes, that's a good idea.'

Privately Marisa decided that when the time came she would find an excuse not to join the party. She wasn't exactly eager to be shunted off on to Giselle's father.

True to his word, Blake expressed his intention of the next morning of running her into Calvi after breakfast. She said she could be ready at any time to suit him, but to her dismay Giselle invited herself to accompany them.

'There are just a few things I need,' the other girl declared, 'and it's silly for me to go in by myself when you're already making the journey. I can be ready at ten.'

She wasn't ready until nearly twenty past, but Marisa observed that Blake didn't appear to mind, especially as Giselle looked devastating in sugar pink jeans and a striped black and white shirt with a pink chiffon scarf tying back her hair and matching the rims of her enormous sunglasses. When Marisa and Blake stopped at the stationer's she disappeared into the beauty shop next door, saying: 'Call for me after you've finished your purchases, will you?'

The stationer's had quite a collection of English books for children, and Blake said: 'Choose whatever you think Fiona would enjoy. You know what's likely to appeal to a child of her age better than I do,' so she made a careful selection and then moved over to where he was leafing through a volume devoted to French architecture.

'Finished?' he enquired. 'Don't you want anything for yourself?'

'I don't think so. The English paperbacks are all rather expensive.'

There were a couple of novels she would like to have bought, but she didn't feel justified in splashing on them since the pocket money Leonie paid her didn't go very far and she was determined to hang on to her fare home in case she ever wanted to leave the villa at a moment's notice.

'Have you read this and this?' Blake slipped the very two paperbacks she had been coveting out of the rack, and she hesitated, then said: 'No, I haven't.'

'I think you'd enjoy them.'

He tucked them into her hand as he possessed himself of the books for Fiona, and paying for the lot ushered her out of the shop. He paused on the pavement.

'If you're going to add teaching Fiona to the rest of your duties then you ought to be paid a proper salary.'

'Oh, there's no need for that. If I'm occupying Fiona then it makes no difference whether it's by teaching her or by playing with her, and look at the fringe benefits I get.'

'What do you count as fringe benefits?'

'Living in the villa where I have the freedom of the pool to swim in, and then trips like this one.' She hugged the paperbacks affectionately. 'I've been dying for ages to read these two.'

'If you're so enthusiastic about the gift of a couple of paperbacks then you're easily pleased.'

There was no time for further argument, because at that moment Giselle emerged from the beauty shop with an armful of packages wrapped in silver and lilac striped paper.

'Isn't shopping exhausting?' she said gaily. 'Let's go and recuperate with a drink. There's rather an attractive place round this corner, Blake. Have you discovered it yet?'

'I don't think so,' he answered, but Marisa drew a breath of dismay as she realised they were heading for the bar where Desirée worked, the very last place she wanted to visit. She had managed to dismiss the girl from her mind for the time being, and now she could only hope that Desirée would be too busy to attend to them.

But Marisa's luck was out. Several of the tables were occupied, and as Giselle headed for one in the far corner Desirée moved away from the adjacent one where she had been taking an order and looked straight at Marisa.

'Now what shall I have?' Giselle sank down gracefully into a chair. 'Oh, I know one should always drink the wine of the country, but I do feel that a gin and tonic with plenty of ice would do more for my morale.'

'Then have it by all means,' said Blake. 'What would you like, Marisa?'

'Oh, anything, a glass of white wine,' chose Marisa, wishing she could render herself invisible. She could see Desirée approaching them, and the next moment the girl paused by the table to take Blake's order. She stared boldly at Marisa, and was obviously on the point of saying something until Giselle's surprised glance caused

67

her to turn away.

'What a sullen-looking creature,' remarked Giselle. 'This place has changed, and not for the better. I shan't bother to come again.'

She chattered on, skilfully excluding Marisa from the conversation, until the drinks arrived. Desirée put them down on the table, then said deliberately to Marisa in French: 'My parents are in no better state, *mademoiselle*. If Michel could see them—'

Giselle stared at her, then at Marisa. 'Do you know this girl, Marisa?'

'Oh, Mademoiselle knows me,' said Desirée with emphasis. 'I was to have married her brother.' She stood there until someone beckoned her from another table, then she walked away.

'Well!' said Giselle expressively. 'I gathered this was a bar you would rather have avoided, Marisa, but how was I to know that? I'd no idea you had a brother out here.'

'I haven't—now,' answered Marisa steadily. 'He was stationed here in the Foreign Legion, but he died some months ago.'

'I'm so sorry.' Giselle was all sympathy. 'It must have been very painful for you to come out here yourself.'

'I'd rather not talk about it, if you don't mind,' said Marisa. She had no intention of discussing her private affairs with Giselle, though she was afraid the damage was done.

'No, I quite understand. Blake, what about a drive this evening when it's cooler? We could go as far as Algajola.'

Giselle made no further reference to the meeting with Desirée, but at the first opportunity after they returned to the villa she sought out Leonie and confessed wryly that she had embarrassed Marisa that morning.

'The very last thing I wanted to do, of course, and no one was more taken aback than I was when this waitress joined in the conversation.'

'I suppose I ought to have told you of the circumstances which brought Marisa out here, but even so I didn't know in which bar this girl was employed.' Leonie went on to explain the situation, ending with: 'Blake advised Marisa not to do anything in a hurry but wait and see what had developed by the end of the summer.'

'I should have thought that if this girl is trying to extort money from her Marisa would be well advised to go home as soon as possible.'

'Blake thinks it may only be a try-on, and it did seem a pity for Marisa not to extend her stay once she'd paid her fare out here. And there's no doubt she has a real knack with Fiona. If Marisa goes I'll have to play nursemaid, and that's the last thing I want.'

'Yes,' said Giselle thoughtfully. 'When are you expecting Jon?'

'Next weekend, providing some financial crisis doesn't crop up to keep him in England. You know what Jon is— the job comes before anything else.'

'Oh, surely not. He's devoted to you and Fiona.'

'He's generous enough, but he doesn't seem to understand what a boring life I lead. He hates going to parties, and he never wants to entertain any but our oldest friends. Sometimes I think I'll go crazy.'

'While he's here I'm sure he'll relax and forget about the bank. You remember we talked of making up a party to visit the Beau Séjour? When you mentioned waiting for Daddy I'd forgotten about Jon; he could be the third man.'

'Marisa will suit Jon admirably since she's so fond of Fiona.'

'Then that's settled, and now I must go and put on a new face for lunch.'

Skilfully applying eyeshadow, Giselle mentally filed away what she had learned about Marisa today. You never knew when information might come in useful, and the fact that Desirée had her own game to play could perhaps be turned to advantage at some time.

By the following weekend, when Blake drove to the airport to meet his brother, Marisa had completely recovered from her accident. Leonie had declared that she would much prefer to stay at the villa to greet her husband since the journey to Bastia would be hot and exhausting, and she was lazing by the pool as usual when the car returned. Rather perfunctorily she rose from her chair as a tall, thin man with lines of strain on his face emerged from the villa on to the terrace.

'Hallo, Jon,' she said casually. 'How are you?'

'Glad of a break. Darling, you're looking very fit. Where's Fiona?'

'At the far end of the garden with Marisa. I didn't tell her you were coming today because I didn't want her to get too excited.'

'Then I'll go and find her. Who's Marisa?'

'Oh, Jon, I'm sure I mentioned her in a letter. She's been staying here and helping me with Fiona.'

'Sorry, darling, I realise now she's the girl who took Sue's place.'

He walked quickly towards the trees, calling: 'Fiona!' and Marisa, hearing him, said to the little girl: 'Someone's calling you; don't you know who it is?'

Fiona listened, then scrambled to her feet, shouting: 'Daddy, Daddy, I'm here!' until he appeared when she ran towards him.

He picked her up and swung her high while she squealed delightedly, crying: 'Do it again, Daddy. Are you going to stay here now?'

'For a little while,' he said. 'Have you missed me?'

'Yes, I have, but Marisa reads me stories like you used to do.'

'Does she?' He turned towards Marisa with a smile, and she felt her heart warm to the tall man with the kind mouth who was like and yet so unlike his brother. 'Thank you for looking after Fiona.'

'It's been very rewarding,' Marisa assured him. 'She knows all her letters now and she's done some very good

70

drawings. She's been keeping them to show you.'

'Come and see them, Daddy.' Fiona tugged at his hand, and he said: 'We must go back to Mummy first.'

'And I can swim too, Daddy.' Fiona danced beside him as they walked back to the pool. 'Marisa taught me.'

'Marisa seems to be responsible for a lot. We'll go in the water, shall we, and you can show me all you've learned.'

'Your husband seems devoted to Fiona,' remarked Marisa to Leonie as she watched father and daughter splashing happily together.

'They've always been very close, but it's easy for Jon, he doesn't have to have her all day and every day. I'm fond of her, but children are so demanding. I'm a person in my own right, not just a wife and mother.'

Presently Giselle appeared, and Jon came out of the pool to greet her.

'Where's Blake?' she asked, and Jon answered: 'Working in the studio, I imagine.'

'Well, he can't be allowed to shut himself up there on your first evening here. I've told Jean to put a bottle of champagne on ice; we must celebrate.'

Giselle disappeared to return in a few minutes with Blake. It was impossible to guess whether he resented being disturbed; if he did he concealed it successfully. They were a gay party at dinner with Giselle sparkling and Jon obviously happy to be reunited with his family again. When the coffee was drunk Giselle suggested driving along the coast to a hotel she knew which overlooked the sea.

'I'll stay with Fiona,' offered Marisa at once.

'I'd be glad if you would,' accepted Leonie with relief. 'I could ask Marie to baby-sit, but I don't like to bother her too much.'

Blake made no move to veto this suggestion, which was understandable. Five was an awkward number and Giselle would certainly have resented Marisa's inclusion in the party. It served to pinpoint the girl's isolation,

71

however, and when they had gone her mind focused on Desirée Roland. Would Michael have wished her to have his inheritance even though they hadn't been able to marry? Marisa tried to come to some decision about this, but in the end found herself shelving it again, though sooner or later it would have to be resolved.

During the next few days Jon devoted himself to Fiona who, however, insisted that Marisa should join in their activities so that she found hself being thrust into Jon's company willy-nilly. Leonie made no objection to this, and spent each afternoon in Calvi where it seemed likely she was meeting Roger. Marisa herself much preferred Jon. He might not be as ebullient as Roger, but she divined character behind his quiet manner and she appreciated his love for and his patience with his little daughter. The more time she spent with him the more she liked him, and couldn't understand why Leonie should appear so indifferent. At first Jon made every attempt to draw his wife into the little circle, but when she resisted he quietly abandoned his efforts and they saw very little of each other apart from mealtimes.

On the Thursday Roger called to announce that the following night there was to be a typical Corsican evening laid on at a little restaurant he knew of up in the mountains.

'It's a tourist attraction, of course,' he admitted, 'but I think you'd enjoy it. If you want to go I'll have to let the proprietor know in advance, because the numbers are strictly limited.'

'Shall we risk it?' queried Giselle lightly. 'It might be rather fun.'

Her eyes were fixed on Blake, who answered: 'Why not?'

'Yes, I agree,' said Jon unexpectedly. 'Book a party of six, will you, Dacre?'

'Six?' Giselle's tone was interrogative, then she continued smoothly: 'But of course Marisa must come too.'

'Certainly she must,' said Jon firmly, and Leonie

broke in: 'Marie can keep an ear open for Fiona.'

It was arranged that they should take two cars, and Marisa felt a pleasurable thrill at the prospect of an evening out. However, she had nothing very suitable to wear, and when Leonie announced that she was driving into Calvi the next morning to have her hair done Marisa begged a lift so that she could look at the shops.

She offered to take Fiona with her, but Jon said: 'No. She and I will find plenty to do together and you can do your shopping in peace.'

There was a boutique in a cobbled street behind the sea-front which Marisa had noticed on a previous visit, so she made straight for this. The dresses displayed in the window were attractive, particularly a full-length sprigged cotton with a low square neckline and bishop sleeves. It was by no means cheap, but it fitted her perfectly except for being slightly too long, so feeling rather reckless she decided to buy it. It would mean that she would have to economise for the next week or two, but the pattern of deep blue flowers and pale green leaves on a white background suited her so well that she couldn't resist it. She spent the afternoon shortening the dress, and was very pleased with the result.

After a herbal shampoo and a vigorous brushing her hair gleamed like chestnut silk, complementing the green eyeshadow and frosted coral lipstick she applied with care. Fortunately her white sandals would pass muster for evening wear, so she smoothed on the dress, picked up a white woollen shawl to serve as a wrap, and went down to join the others.

It was a foregone conclusion that Giselle would travel in Blake's car, so Marisa wasn't surprised to find herself sitting in the back of Roger's car with Leonie installed in the front. Jon seemed to approve of this arrangement too, because he put himself out to entertain her by chatting about life in London and asking her if she were fond of music and the theatre. The road to the mountains led over a stone bridge, then she became aware of

73

the scent of the *maquis* on the night air and the clusters
of lights round the bay below. There was a deep golden
moon suspended in the sky which lent an air of enchantment to the whole scene.

The road wound up and up until at last they came to
a tiny village where the houses elbowed each other round
a square in the centre of which stood the church, its bell
tower rearing into the sky. Roger parked to one side of
the church and Blake drew up beside him, Roger explaining when he got out of the car that the alleyway where the
cave was situated was too narrow to take wheeled traffic.

'Where on earth are we going?' queried Giselle as they
found thsemselves stumbling over cobbles in almost total
darkness. The only lights gleamed from behind the shut-
tered windows of the houses, then suddenly a brilliant
glow spilled out from an open door and they had
arrived.

The room where they were to dine had been roughly
scooped out of the rock itself, but had been made
attractive by dazzlingly whitewashed walls and a scarlet
ceiling. Two wooden steps led down into the room which
had a tiled floor and was filled by long wooden tables
and stout country chairs, the tables being covered with
red cotton cloths. The bar was a high wooden affair with
bottles stacked behind it, and at the back of the room a
doorway led into a dark kitchen from which came a
delicious smell of herbs and meat. The long tables were
already partly filled and Roger led his party to the end
of one of them, joking: 'Exactly like a Sunday school
treat, isn't it?'

The warm friendly atmosphere was very much to
Marisa's taste even though she was conscious of being
outshone by both Giselle and Leonie. Giselle was wearing a long black skirt and a silver top which fitted her
like a second skin. Both garments were perfectly plain
but unmistakably expensive, and even Leonie's peacock
silk shot with gold couldn't rival them. Faced with these
two exotic creations Marisa's sprigged cotton looked
74

completely unsophisticated, but she comforted herself
with the thought that at least it fitted her and the colours
were becoming.

A plump country girl came round with glasses of per-
nod, and Marisa sipped cautiously at the cloudy liquid.
She didn't care very much for the aniseed taste, but the
drink gave her an appetite for the vegetable soup which
was now being ladled from a huge tureen.

The food was plentiful and good, the soup being
followed by thin slices of raw smoked ham with a salad
of tomatoes, lettuce, cucumber and green peppers, then
a ragout of mutton thick with potatoes, onions, carrots
and spiced with herbs. After this came hard pungent
white cheese served on flat green leaves and baskets of
fresh fruit, all washed down with as much local red wine
as could be drunk. When no one could eat any more
there was a rush of people from the kitchen to clear the
tables and fold them away, leaving the floor free for
dancing.

Now a record player was trundled in and soon everyone was on their feet. Marisa found herself partnering
Jon, Roger and Blake in turn, then being claimed by
perfect strangers. The temperature in the low room rose
until she felt she couldn't endure another moment without a breath of fresh air, and pushing through the crowd
to the door she stumbled out into the alleyway.

Moonlight was flooding the landscape, and she stood
for a few seconds revelling in the cool air before making
her way along the alley to the open square. Once out of
the shadow of the church it was as bright as day, and she
walked over to the low wall bounding the square on one
side to gaze down into the valley below. There were clusters of lights like tiny jewels and not a sound to be heard
except for the faint whisper of the breeze in the trees, so
that she gave a gasp of alarm when Blake's voice behind
her said: 'You shouldn't be wandering out here alone,
Marisa. Suppose I intended to snatch your bag, I'd only
have to give you a push and you'd be down there among

75

the rocks with no one the wiser.'

She gave a shudder and answered: 'Don't be so grue-some! It was so hot in there I simply had to have some fresh air.'

'Then you should have asked Jon or myself to come out with you.'

'That never occurred to me. Isn't it a lovely night and a wonderful view?'

They sood there in silence, and it was as if there were no one else in the world. Marisa became intensely aware of the man so close beside her, and gave way to an un-controllable impulse to turn and look at him. He held her gaze, and then as her breath began to come faster he slid his hands up her arms to pull her towards him. It was a swift kiss, so soon over that she had only a con-fused recollection of the firm pressure of his lips on hers when he released her.

'Come along,' he said. 'It's time we went back to the others.'

Dazedly she moved forward, and he cupped his hand under her elbow as he guided her across the square and along the alleyway. Neither of them noticed a figure melt into the shadow cast by the buttress of the church or dis-covered when they returned to the noisy crowded room that Giselle was also missing. She had seen Blake leave and followed him, meaning to get him to herself in the moonlight, but before she could catch up with him he had joined Marisa. Giselle saw that kiss, and her hand clenched round a projecting piece of stonework until her fingers were white. A kiss meant nothing these days, but she regarded Blake as her property and intended to eliminate any opposition before it became serious. She couldn't imagine him falling for such an insignificant female as Marisa Farnham, but men were unpredictable. If she had any reason to suspect Marisa as a rival for Blake's affections then she would have to take steps. That girl in the restaurant who had declared that Marisa's brother intended to marry her might prove very useful in the future. Giselle strolled thoughtfully back to the *cave*, her brain working busily.

CHAPTER V

Back dancing to the music of the record player, Marisa found it impossible to believe that Blake had actually kissed her. It must have been the effect of the moonlight, she assured herself, though she had never suspected he could be influenced by his surroundings, however romantic. The fact remained that she was unable to forget that kiss, and when she was back in her room at the villa she switched off the light and opened the window, leaning out over the sill to breathe in the perfume of the *maquis* which was always present. Finally, reluctantly remembering that Fiona would be awake and lively soon after seven, she slid into bed, only to be awakened from a sound sleep by Fiona tugging at her insistently and commanding her to get up.

She pulled on slacks and a thin sweater, then took the little girl down to breakfast where Blake was drinking a cup of coffee while reading a letter. He greeted them abstractedly so that more than ever the events of the previous evening seemed incredible, and as soon as his cup was empty excused himself and disappeared. The flatness of the morning after the night before descended on Marisa, and she had to force herself to greet Jon cheerfully when he came on to the terrace a moment later.

He also seemed more preoccupied than usual, and Marisa sensed that it was an effort for him to respond to Fiona's liveliness.

'Finish your breakfast, Daddy, and then we can go into the garden to play,' demanded the little girl, but he shook his head.

'Not this morning, sweetheart, I've things to do.'

Fiona's mouth drooped. 'But I want you to swim with me in the pool.'

'I'll swim with you,' interposed Marisa.

'Don't want you, I want Daddy to swim with me.'

'Don't be a baby, Fiona,' said Jon sharply.

He so very rarely rebuked her that she stared at him in consternation, then the tears welled up in her eyes and she opened her mouth to howl. Marisa, realising that Jon was in no mood to endure a scene, picked her up and whisked her off the terrace and into the garden, where she cried hard for two minutes and then for want of an audience dried up.

'Finished?' enquired Marisa briskly. 'Now what about that swim in the pool?'

Fiona had soon forgotten her troubles, but Marisa noticed that Jon was still silent at lunch and that Leonie was also very offhand. Had they had a row? the girl wondered, and speculated still more when Leonie drove out in the car. Giselle suggested to Blake that he should accompany her into Ile-Rousse where she wanted to patronise a particular shop and that they should stay to have dinner there. When he agreed but said he wouldn't be free until three o'clock she announced that she would have a siesta first in her room.

'It's too hot on the terrace today,' she declared. 'There isn't a breath of wind.'

Marisa, who usually sat in the garden or on the terrace herself while Fiona had her nap, also decided to go to her own room where it would be cooler. She curled up in a chair with the window opened wide and was feeling drowsy when the sound of voices in the garden roused her.

She heard Jon say: 'Blake, can you spare me a moment?' and Blake's reply: 'It can only be a moment. As you know, I'm taking Giselle out at three and I've something to finish first.'

'It's Leonie,' said Jon dispiritedly. 'We seem to have drifted so far apart that we've no point of contact. We need to talk, but I can't get her to myself in the daytime and at night she pleads tiredness and goes straight to sleep, or pretends to.'

'You thought things would be better if you had a break from each other.'

'Yes, I did, that's why I asked you to invite her to share the villa with you, but it hasn't worked out as I'd hoped. Will you do me a favour and ensure that I get a few uninterrupted hours alone with Leonie by taking the others on a trip somewhere?'

'I could do—if you think it would help.'

' I think it might, at any rate I'm desperate enough to try anything. For Fiona's sake I can't let my marriage just fall to pieces.'

'If we went to Porto that would be an all-day excursion, but suppose Leonie wants to come too?'

'I'll see she doesn't get the chance to go. As you know, she's never up before ten, so if you set off at nine—'

'I expect we can manage that.'

The two men separated, and Marisa reflected on what she had unwittingly heard. It hadn't surprised her to learn of the estrangement between Jon and his wife, but she sincerely hoped that they could come together again. Because of that she responded enthusiastically to Blake's suggestion the next morning that they should drive to Porto the following day.

'I'd love to see it,' she said, and Giselle remarked: 'It's a beautiful place and an enchanting drive to reach it. Are we all going, Blake?'

'Not Leonie and Jon, they're having a day to themselves. There'll just be the four of us—you and I, Marisa and Fiona.'

'Oh, don't you think it will be too hot and tiring for Fiona? She'd really be much better off in the garden by the pool.'

'I don't think it will hurt her for once,' responded

79

Blake easily, 'and between us we ought to be able to keep her amused.'

'Of course. I was only considering what would be best for her, but if you want her to go——'

'This time I do.'

Giselle smiled prettily. 'Then there's no more to be said.'

Cleverly Blake and Jon between them managed to ensure that the expedition to Porto wasn't mentioned in Leonie's presence, and when the party assembled at breakfast she was still in bed. Fiona was in high spirits, and Marisa noticed Giselle's mouth tighten once, but the other woman managed to keep her temper.

The morning was faintly misty, giving promise of a hot day, and the scenery was spectacular enough to keep Marisa craning her neck from side to side. As the car sped along the mountains rose sheer, layer upon layer, and the air was heavy with the fragrance of rosemary, myrtle and cistus. As the sun grew hotter the shade of the magnificent sweet chestnut trees was welcome, and when they drove past the Foreign Legion outpost Marisa thought of Michael and wondered if he had ever visited this spot.

Then they came to the Col de Vergio, the highest road summit in Corsica. Blake stopped the car and they all got out, but it was so bitterly cold that they were glad to scramble back. Giselle shuddered, and said: 'Oh, why did I disturb myself? I'm quite frozen!'

'Sorry,' said Blake, 'but we'll stop quite soon for an early lunch.'

'At that little bar-restaurant perched on top of the cliffs?'

'Yes. I thought it would be a good place because Fiona can run about there.'

Blake turned to Marisa. 'On the return journey I thought we'd go a little way south so that you can see Les Calanches. They're unique.'

The bar-restaurant Giselle had mentioned was situated

almost on the edge of the cliff overlooking the sea and boasted a vine-covered terrace edged with pots of red and pink geraniums. They ate omelettes made with *brocciu*, the delicious white cheese of Corsica, followed by fresh fruit, and it was while the others were drinking a local red wine and Fiona was enjoying a *sirop* that she saw the monkey. He was wearing red trousers with a yellow jacket, and he darted out of the door of the restaurant to climb swiftly up an umbrella pine where he swung from one of the lower branches.

'Oh, look, Marisa,' cried Fiona rapturously, 'isn't he lovely? Can I pick him up, Uncle Blake?'

'If you can catch him,' said Blake amusedly, and Fiona ran to the pine tree, whereupon the monkey chattered incomprehensibly and leaped on to a higher branch. Fiona was fascinated and crouched under the tree, making coaxing noises to persuade him to come down.

Blake said: 'I'm going along to the car to consult a map, so you might as well take it easy for the next ten minutes. By the way, there's a small shop attached to the restaurant, Marisa, if you're looking for souvenirs. It usually stocks one or two decent things carved out of olive wood.'

'If you like that kind of thing,' yawned Giselle, and leaned back in her chair.

Blake disappeared and Marisa looked at Fiona, who was completely absorbed in the monkey, then said: 'I'd like to look at the shop if you're staying here, Giselle. Will you keep an eye on Fiona?'

Giselle nodded, and Marisa made her way through the bead curtain at the entrance to the restaurant into the shop on the left. It was quite small but boasted a variety of goods, among them platters and cheeseboards cut to display the grain of the olive wood. Marisa, having decided to buy something she could use every day to remind her of this holiday, examined the cheeseboards and finally chose one which had a very pleasing grain. When she had paid for it she went out into the sunlight

81

again, to find Giselle still sitting on the terrace, but no sign at all of Fiona.

As she reached Giselle she noticed that the other girl's eyes were closed, and with a quick stab of alarm she cried: 'Where's Fiona? Is she with Blake?'

'What?' murmured Giselle sleepily, and opened her eyes. 'Oh, the sun's so hot that I believe I must have dozed off.'

'Where's Fiona? I left her in your charge. You said you'd keep an eye on her.'

'You're mistaken. I'd no idea she wasn't with you. After all, you're supposed to be looking after her.'

'Yes, but I told you I was going to the shop and asked you to keep an eye on her. You nodded, so I assumed you'd heard what I said.'

'If you thought I nodded you were completely mistaken. I'd no idea you'd gone away.'

Realising she was only wasting time by arguing, Marisa ran to the edge of the terrace, then down the two shallow steps leading on to the drive and into the road. As she glanced frantically either way, hoping to catch a glimpse of Fiona's pink frock, she saw Blake walking up from the car park further down the lane and flew towards him.

'Have you see Fiona?' she gasped. 'I went into the shop to look at the souvenirs and when I came out she'd gone. I asked Giselle to watch Fiona, but she says she never heard me.'

'When I left Fiona was absorbed in the antics of the monkey; she can't have strayed far.'

Marisa turned deathly pale. 'There's no sign of the monkey either. You don't think—'

She cast a terrified glance to where the edge of the road tumbled steeply down into a thicket of bushes. 'If anything's happened to her I'll never forgive myself!'

'Spare me the dramatics,' said Blake harshly, 'and let's concentrate on finding her. You go to the left and I'll go to the right.'

At that moment Giselle appeared, a look of concern on her face.

'Have you found her?' she called.

Marisa flew past her. 'Not yet.'

She began to call: 'Fiona, Fiona!' and rapidly scanned the undergrowth on one side of the road. The other side was a sheer rock face which no one, not even a goat, could have scaled.

Marisa, ran on, calling constantly, then just when she judged there hadn't been time for Fiona to get any further and was about to turn back she heard a faint cry. She peered over the edge of the path into the *maquis* but could see nothing, then the cry came again and on her right she thought she caught a glimpse of pink among the bushes. She moved in the direction of it, then lay flat to look down. There below her Fiona had been trapped and held in a large bush a few feet down the cliff.

The little girl wailed again, and Marisa called: 'Don't move, darling, and we'll soon have you up again.'

She stretched down as far as she dared, but there was no hope of reaching Fiona unless she climbed down to her and that would leave them both stranded. She must get help, so loath as she was to leave the child, she jumped to her feet, and calling reassuringly: 'I'll be back in a moment,' she began to run along the road as fast as she could. It was still very hot so that her shirt clung to her and her hair was plastered in damp wisps on her forehead. When at last she saw Blake and Giselle coming towards her she was too breathless to speak.

At last she managed to gasp: 'I've found Fiona. She must have fallen over the edge of the cliff, but fortunately she was caught by some bushes a little way down. I tried to reach her, but I couldn't.'

Blake wasted no breath on words but began to run to the spot she pointed out and Marisa followed. When she reached him he was assessing the situation, then he turned to her.

'I'll climb down to Fiona and if she isn't hurt I'll lift

83

her on to my shoulders. If I do that I think the two of you ought to be able to reach her and pull her up. Do you think you can manage that?'

'Yes,' said Marisa resolutely, 'but do be careful. If you should slip—'

Blake began to lower himself over the edge. 'Don't worry, I shall be all right.'

Giselle shuddered. 'I daren't even look. I've no head for heights at all,' and she stood well back in the road.

Marisa lay flat and watched Blake test each foothold as he worked his way down to where Fiona lay. Fortunately the bushes had thick tough roots, but Marisa was racked by anxiety as he took the strain on his toes and fingertips. At last he reached Fiona and smiled reassuringly at her.

'We'll soon have you at the top, chicken. Isn't it a good thing that there's a nice ledge here where I can stand? If I bend down do you think you can stretch out your hand very gently and grasp mine? That's it; now on to my knee and up on to my shoulder. Hold tight while I straighten up.'

With one supple movement Blake was upright and facing the cliff with Fiona sitting on his shoulders.

He said calmly: 'Can you reach her, Marisa?' and Marisa stretched down towards the little girl.

'Not quite,' she panted. 'Giselle, hold on to my feet while I move a few inches forward.'

Giselle grasped her ankles and Marisa leaned farther out over the cliff edge.

'Be careful,' warned Giselle. 'You've heavier than I am, and if you began to slip I couldn't hold you.'

Blake braced himself against the cliff and lifted Fiona a little higher while Marisa leaned forward again and this time managed to grasp Fiona's wrists. She tried to haul the little girl up bodily while every one of her muscles screamed a protest, but the effort was too great.

'I can't do it,' she croaked. 'She's too heavy.'

'Can you hang on to her while I climb up and help

you,' asked Blake calmly. 'I can fix her feet in two holds here which will take some of the strain off your arms, and I'll be as quick as I can.'

'I'll hang on,' said Marisa through her teeth. She tried to smile. 'Don't worry, Fiona, I won't let go of you. Just keep still and in a very few minutes we'll pull you up.'

She felt as if her arms were being wrenched from their sockets as Blake began his upward climb, but she continued to talk to Fiona until at last he heaved himself over the edge. lying down beside her and covering her hands with his own. Then with one quick jerk Fiona was pulled up.

'Good girl, you can let go of her now,' said Blake softly, but it was a second or two before Marisa could force herself to release the little girl's wrists. Now that the danger was over she was trembling uncontrollably, but Fiona was crying from schock and reaction so Marisa was able to concentrate on comforting her.

'It's all over now,' she soothed, 'but how did you come to fall over the edge?'

'The monkey jumped into another tree,' gulped Fiona, 'so I followed him along the road, then he began to climb down a big bush and when I reached out to grab him I slipped.'

'You knew it was naughty to leave the restaurant garden, didn't you?'

'But you weren't there and she was asleep, and I never thought the monkey would go so far.'

'I think we'd better forget about your narrow escape and see what delights Porto has to offer,' suggested Blake.

'I agree with you,' said Giselle. 'When I think what might have happened it makes me shudder. I don't think I shall ever want to visit this restaurant again.'

Fiona was very subdued as they got into the car, but when they reached Porto with its white sand and sparkling sea she brightened. Marisa thought it was the most beautiful bay she had ever seen with its beach backed by eucalyptus trees and the ruined watch tower perched on a spur of rock.

'Let's just laze in the sun,' suggested Giselle. 'After that heart-stopping episode I don't feel like doing anything strenuous, do you, Blake?'

He smiled at her. 'Not really.'

'Can I paddle?' begged Fiona.

'Yes, of course,' answered Marisa. 'We'll paddle together.'

She kicked off her sandals, and Blake indicated a hotel overlooking the beach.

'We'll be up there on the terrace. Come and join us for a drink when you're ready.'

Giselle slipped her arm through his and they went off together while Marisa took Fiona's hand as she skipped along the beach. There were fascinating plants and pebbles which they stopped to examine, and Fiona had to be dissuaded from collecting them to take home with her. Finally they made their way to the hotel where the other two were sitting with their drinks and as they approached Marisa acknowledged how attractive Giselle looked, being conscious of her own tousled appearance with her hair tossed by the breeze and the bottoms of her jeans stained with sea water from scrambling over the rocks.

Blake ordered her a drink and an ice for Fiona, but it was impossible for her to relax. She couldn't forgive her own carelessness and what might have been the result of it. She had thought that Giselle understood she was leaving Fiona in her charge, but she ought to have made absolutely sure.

After they'd been sitting lazily there for some time Blake said: 'It's a pity to move, but I want to give Marisa a glimpse of Les Calanches before we start back.'

'Yes, they're so spectacular that she really mustn't miss them,' agreed Giselle, so Blake drove south through the great jagged masses of crimson granite cliffs all carved into weird twisted shapes. They were unlike anything Marisa had ever seen before, so that she was spellbound

86

at the effect of the light on them.

'You really ought to see them at sunrise or sunset to get the maximum effect,' Blake told her, 'but we can't linger too long because of Fiona.'

He turned the car towards Calvi and Fiona, tired now, snuggled up against Marisa, who took the little girl on to her lap, thankful that she was safe and unhurt. As they drove along the sea deepened to ultramarine, the setting sun throwing a bar of gold across the water, then they turned inland to come eventually to a tiny café-bar with a shabby terrace crammed with pots of flowers. Blake stretched and said: 'We'll stop here for coffee before we do the last lap.'

Marisa answered: 'I won't bother getting out of the car. Fiona's fallen asleep.'

Ignoring this, Blake opened the rear door and said: 'She'll be perfectly all right if you lay her on the back seat, and you'll be very cramped by the time we arrive home if you don't take this opportunity of moving. Come along.'

Reluctantly Marisa laid Fiona down and followed the other two to the rough chairs and table set out on the terrace, casting several backward glances at the car. Blake ordered coffee and he and Giselle talked to each other. Marisa tried to join in, but Giselle persistently diverted the conversation to personal topics and office gossip about which Marisa knew nothing. Once or twice Blake turned to her to ask her opinion, but each time Giselle cleverly manœuvred the subject back to something of her own choosing.

Finally she said: 'Well, I must go and tidy myself, if this primitive place boasts anything like a ladies' room.'

She sauntered through a door into the bar, Marisa involuntarily glancing at the car again.

Blake said coolly: 'There's no need to be so prostrated with guilt, you know. It could have happened to anyone.'

'But I should have made absolutely certain that Giselle was awake before I left Fiona,' answered Marisa miser-

87

ably. 'If she hadn't been caught by those bushes and had fallen right down the cliff side—'

She shuddered uncontrollably, and Blake said: 'But she didn't, so stop thinking about it. What you need is a brandy.'

'No, nothing more. I'm quite all right now.'

He took no notice of her protests but ordered the brandy and when it came commanded her to drink it. She did so and had to admit that it warmed her through and took away the fluttery feeling in her stomach. She smiled uncertainly at him and he smiled back, saying: 'Good girl, now you'll feel better.'

Giselle came back at that moment looking immaculate, and Marisa realised that she ought to make the effort to tidy herself, but couldn't be bothered. What did it matter? Her looks would never rival Giselle's however hard she tried. The brandy had made her sleepy, so back in the car she put her arms round Fiona who hadn't stirred a muscle and drifted off to sleep herself. The next thing she was aware of was a hand on her shoulder, shaking her, and a voice saying: 'Wake up, we're home.'

She blinked and looked up into Blake's face, trying to focus on it. Fiona stirred as Blake took her out of Marisa's arms to hand her to Jean, then helped Marisa out of the car. She stumbled, holding on to him for support, feeling the warmth of his body and the hardness of the muscles under her grasp.

Giselle said amusedly: 'You and Fiona are a good pair. You've missed all the exciting scenery on the way back,' making Marisa feel foolish and naïve.

She loosed her hold on Blake's arm immediately, but he put his hand under her elbow to hold it firmly. Marisa was too dazed to notice the effect the gesture had on the other girl, but Giselle's lips tightened and she stalked ahead of them into the villa in a very unamiable frame of mind.

Fiona flew to her father, eager to tell him of her adventure now that all danger was passed, and Marisa said apologetically: 'I hope you'll forgive me for leaving her.'

With one arm round his daughter Jon said: 'You're too hard on yourself; I'm sure you weren't to blame. Come along, sweetheart, it's long past your bedtime. I'll take you up.'

It was impossible to tell from his demeanour whether the day had been profitable for him or not. Leonie seemed unchanged, neither more nor less friendly to her husband than usual, but when she and Marisa met on the landing after dinner she quickly showed that she was quite alive to what had been going on.

She enquired: 'How did you like Porto?' and Marisa answered: 'I thought it was beautiful. Blake made a detour to show me Les Calanches; they're incredible, aren't they?'

'Yes, quite fantastic. You were all very secretive about this trip. I notice I wasn't offered the chance to go.'

'I think it was all decided very much on the spur of the moment.'

'You don't need to pretend. I'm convinced it was engineered by Blake to give Jon and me the opportunity to be alone together and resolve our differences.'

'He said nothing of that to me.'

'He wouldn't; he believes in family loyalty. Oh, Jon's unselfish and worthy and I'm lucky to have him for a husband, but that's the trouble. He's too good and it makes him dull. Now with Roger I always feel on top of the world; he's fun.'

'But in a crisis I'm sure Jon would always emerge triumphant. He's so stable and understanding.'

'You should be his P.R. man,' said Leonie flippantly. 'You're probably right, but life isn't a constant crisis.'

'You wouldn't leave Jon for Roger?'

'I don't know. So far I haven't been faced with a decision because I haven't encouraged Roger, in spite of what you all think, but when the end of this holiday approaches—well, I honestly don't know.'

'But there's Fiona to consider.'

'I'm entitled to be considered too,' said Leonie violently. 'Fiona was a mistake—I never intended to start a family so soon—and I don't propose to be handicapped for the rest of my life by her. Blake's no need to be so self-righteous; he's been keeping Giselle dangling for long enough. I suppose he's waiting to see if his Town Centre design gets the award before he proposes. Why do the Wantage men have to be so conscientious?'

She tossed her head and ran down the stairs while Marisa made to follow her and then drew back. She hadn't much inclination to go down to the others again and make polite conversation. It had been a long day and trying in parts, so she would be glad of an early night.

She followed out this plan, so saw nobody until breakfast the next morning. When she walked on to the terrace Blake was drinking a solitary cup of coffee.

'Hallo,' he said. 'What are your plans for today?'

'I haven't any,' confessed Marisa.

'Why don't you take Fiona to the beach on the far side of Calvi bay? You can borrow my car; I shall be working all day.'

'Oh, I'm sure she'd love that, but would you trust me with your car?'

'Why not?' he countered amusedly. 'You're not likely to go berserk when you get your hands on the wheel, are you?'

'Hardly. After that fright yesterday I'm bound to be doubly careful today.'

'Why do you blame yourself so bitterly for what happened? It was only a momentary lapse—if that.'

'But I ought to have made sure that Giselle knew I was leaving Fiona in her charge.'

'Ah, yes.'

There was a curious inflection in his voice which Marisa couldn't interpret, and then he rose to his feet.

'The car's in the garage and here are the keys. Have a good day.'

Left to herself, Marisa poured out a cup of coffee and

nibbled a roll. It was kind of Blake to lend her the car and she would enjoy spending the day on the beach with Fiona. Perhaps she could induce Marie to give them a picnic lunch. Fiona was overjoyed at the prospect in store and needed no prompting to eat her breakfast.

When she and Marisa were seated in the car she said: 'Yesterday there were four of us, weren't there, and now it's just you and me.'

'So it is,' agreed Marisa, startled to discover how much she wished Blake was with them at that moment, and firmly putting all thought of him out of her mind.

Giselle breakfasted late on nothing but a cup of coffee and a cigarette. She inhaled deeply, her mind working busily. It was laughable to suppose that a whey-faced creature like Marisa Farnham could ever be a rival for Blake's affections, but there was no sense in taking risks. Marisa must be eliminated, but unobtrusively, of course, and she had an idea about that. Giselle stubbed out her cigarette and went back to her room to change into a trouser suit of rose pink linen and a dark crimson shirt. When she came down again she went to the garage and was soon driving along the road which led to Calvi.

Arriving in the town she parked her car and sauntered away from the front in the direction of the restaurant where Desirée Roland was employed. Reaching it, she descended the flight of steps into the courtyard and sat down at one of the small tables. Only one other was occupied, and she seated herself as far away from it as possible. She wanted privacy for her conversation.

In a moment Desirée appeared and came across to take her order.

'I should like a pastis,' said Giselle in French, and eyed the girl critically. The sulky mouth and ripe figure confirmed her previous judgement. Desirée Roland would be a very handy tool.

'You are the girl who was going to marry the Englishman, aren't you?' she asked. 'What a pity it all came to nothing.'

91

A heavy sullen look spread over Desirée's face. 'He assured me of a fine home and that my parents should live in comfort too. His sister should fulfil that promise, Bernard says so. It was not my fault Michel died.'

'It does seem rather hard on you,' commiserated Giselle. 'Who is Bernard?'

'He owns this restaurant.'

'He is your lover?'

'Of course not. He advises me, that is all.'

And would expect a cut if Desirée's hopes were realised, thought Giselle shrewdly. Aloud she said: 'But Miss Farnham refuses to give you anything?'

'She pretended to consider the matter, but I have heard nothing further.'

'Then I think it would be wise to remind her. Did you know that her uncle left her his money?'

'Then some of it should be mine,' breathed Desirée avidly. 'If all had gone well by now I would have been the wife of her brother.'

'Very true, and in your place I should approach Miss Farnham. She is staying at the Villa Beaugency, four miles outside the town on the road to Algajola. There is no need to mention this conversation.'

Desirée nodded, and Giselle, having finished her pastis, dropped a few coins on the table and walked away very satisfied with the result of her manœuvre, quite sure that Desirée would react predictably to it.

The following afternoon Marisa was in the garden with Fiona when Jean came to tell her that there was a person asking for her.

'A—a woman, *mademoiselle*,' he explained, casting an eye at Giselle and Leonie who were both stretched out in long chairs by the pool.

'I can't imagine who it can be,' said Marisa, and Leonie instructed lazily: 'Ask her to come into the sitting-room, Jean. You can see her there, Marisa.'

'Very good, *madame*,' said Jean, and Marisa followed him into the house. In a moment he returned ushering

Desirée before him, a Desirée who looked more volup-
tuous than ever in a short tight black skirt and a pink satin
blouse.

Marisa's heart sank when she saw her visitor, because
she was no nearer coming to a decision about what to do
than she had been when they first met.

Feeling a hypocrite, she said: 'Good afternoon, what
can I do for you?'

Her French had become much more fluent over the
past weeks since she had been practising it with Jean,
whom she had grown to like and who had proved very
helpful, and now she spoke to Desirée in her own
language.

The other girl's expression was calculating as she
replied: 'I think you know that very well, *mademoiselle*. I
need help for my parents. My mother is infirm; she
requires good nourishing food, but we have little money
to buy it. I was to have married your brother and he had
promised to treat my parents as if they were his own. I am
here now to beg for them because your brother spoke to
me of you many times, of how close you were to each
other as children.'

That was true, and Marisa felt mean and despicable for
hesitating, yet she couldn't warm to Desirée. She had a
feeling that the other girl was playing a part, though she
certainly had proof that Michael had been in love with
her. If so he would have wanted his sister to help her,
and once again Marisa found herself torn between her
instinct and her conscience.

She said truthfully: 'I can't help you now, Desirée,
even if I wanted to, since I haven't any money.'

'But you have money in England, the money your
uncle left to you.'

'Who told you that?'

Desirée shrugged. 'One hears these things.'

Marisa supposed that was true. She had spoken of her
affairs only to Blake and Leonie, but it would have been
easy enough for Jean or Marie to overhear what she had

said and to repeat it outside the villa. Now Desirée had the advantage, and it wouldn't be easy to fob her off.

'I can't do anything at the moment,' repeated Marisa. 'I should have to get in touch with my solicitors to have money sent out from England.'

'Then I will call again,' said Desirée. 'There is no need for you to inconvenience yourself by coming to the restaurant, *mademoiselle*.'

She flounced across the room and into the hall where Jean appeared, ready to show her out. Marisa watched her leave, unhappily conscious that Desirée intended to present herself again and again at the villa until she got what she came for.

Jean hesitated, and then said sympathetically: 'Do not have dealings with such a one, *mademoiselle*. She is up to no good.'

'I wish I could follow your advice, Jean,' replied Marisa wryly, and returned to the garden where Leonie looked up to say: 'Who was your mysterious visitor?'

'Desirée Roland,' answered Marisa reluctantly.

'That girl who was going to marry your brother? How did she know where you were staying?'

'I've no idea, but it wouldn't be difficult for her to find out.'

'I should send her packing,' yawned Leonie. 'She must realise you can't be bound by your brother's promises.'

'It won't be easy to convince her of that. Unfortunately she's heard my uncle left his money to me.'

Leonie grimaced. 'Oh, dear!'

'I do hope she isn't going to make a nuisance of herself by calling here constantly,' said Giselle sharply. 'Those kind of people are terribly persistent, and I don't want her hanging round the villa.'

Marisa flushed uncomfortably. She could appreciate Giselle's point of view, and the fact that she herself was an employee at the villa made matters doubly awkward. She was spared from having to reply by a yell from Fiona who had fallen and grazed her knee, and in attending to the little girl Marisa temporarily forgot about Desirée.

When she had changed as usual into a dress for dinner she came down to the terrace and stood looking out over the garden. Jean appeared with a tray of glasses, and then with a side glance he said carefully: 'You look a little tired, *mademoiselle*. Let me pour you an aperitif.'

'Thank you, Jean, I'll have a Dubonnet,' answered Marisa, and when he had mixed it he handed it to her, saying: 'Forgive me, *mademoiselle*, but your visitor this afternoon, do you know her well?'

'Scarcely at all,' answered Marisa, and then on impulse she added: 'You have heard about my brother, I expect, Jean. He was stationed here in the Foreign Legion, and he would have married that girl you saw this afternoon if he had lived.'

'So I had heard, *mademoiselle*, but I have also heard other rumours. My wife is a Corsican, but I am not—I come from Paris—so I am not intimate with many people here, but still certain things come to my ears. This woman, she is asking you for money?'

'Yes.'

'Do not give her any yet.'

'But if she were to have married my brother I feel she's entitled to something.'

'Wait for a while longer until I have had an opportunity to approach a man I know in Calvi.'

'Very well, Jean, only I must act soon.'

'I understand, *mademoiselle*.'

Three days went by during which Jean made no attempt to contact her so that Marisa guessed he had no information for her as yet. She longed to consult Blake again, but shied away from this, not wanting to inflict her troubles on him since he seemed to be working very hard and spent almost the whole of his time in the studio. Leonie was out as much as ever, sometimes with Giselle and sometimes with Roger, while Jon devoted himself to Fiona so that Marisa had really very little with which to occupy herself. On the fourth day Marie appeared to say that Mademoiselle Roland had called again to see Mademoiselle Farnham, and with a sinking heart Marisa went out into the hall. She was tempted to postpone the encounter, but was sure that Marie had already announced her to be at home, also there was no point in evading Desirée now only to have her call again the next day.

Desirée was leaning against a small table, and didn't trouble to straighten herself as the other girl approached.

She said insolently: 'Here I am once more, *mademoiselle*, as I promised. I have still not heard from you and the situation grows desperate.'

'There hasn't been time for me to hear from my solicitor,' said Marisa more boldly than she felt.

'Then I will call each day to see if a letter has arrived.'

'Oh, no,' said Marisa involuntarily, and Desirée's eyes gleamed with satisfaction.

'But yes, I think, *mademoiselle*.'

'Look,' said Marisa unhappily, 'I will give you twenty francs to buy something for your mother on condition that you stay away for at least another week.'

'Twenty francs, that is nothing,' said Desirée contemptuously.

'It is all I can spare. Wait here.'

Marisa ran to her room, knowing that she was acting foolishly but willing to do anything to buy a little time. She came down with the money and thrust it at Desirée.

'Remember that you are not to come here again. I'll get in touch with you before the week is out.'

'Rest assured that if you do not I shall be back,' said Desirée threateningly, and strolled to the door.

At least no one had seen her this time except Marie, thought Marisa, but her relief was shortlived. She was alone in the garden when Giselle returned from a trip into Calvi and sought her out, a frown on her face.

'Marie tells me that the Roland girl has been here again,' said Giselle accusingly. 'I mentioned before that I wouldn't have it, and I won't. To prevent her becoming a nuisance there's only one course for you to take. Obviously you'd be stupid to pay her money even if you could afford it, so the only solution is for you to go back to England. She won't follow you there, and you can't pretend you're needed here now. Jon more or less looks after Fiona, so there's nothing for you to do.'

It was true, and besides, she couldn't continue to stay here in Giselle's house if she were unwelcome.

'Very well, I'll enquire about flights and leave as soon as possible,' agreed Marisa, and went up to her room.

She would have to go back to England; she should have gone before this, but she had postponed the decision because she didn't want to leave Corsica. No, she must be strictly honest with herself. It wasn't only that she wanted to stay in Corsica, but that she longed to remain near Blake Wantage. It was ridiculously foolish of her when he was plainly committed to Giselle, but somehow without realising it until now she had given him her heart.

The thought that once she had left the villa she would never see him again made her draw a sharp breath, but she had to steel herself against the pain. Looking back she couldn't decide when her dislike for him had gradually faded and been replaced by love, but the metamorphosis was complete. She loved him warmly and deeply, and was possessed by the unhappy conviction that she could never care for anyone else.

CHAPTER VI

She said nothing about her plans to the others that night, resolving to ring the airport and book on the first available flight to England before announcing her departure. With this on her mind she didn't notice Jean hovering about until she was crossing the hall after dinner, when he intercepted her, murmuring urgently: 'A word with you, *mademoiselle*, about that affair we discussed previously.'

'Oh.' Marisa hesitated. 'I don't know whether it matters now. Have you discovered something?'

'The man I spoke of who lives in Calvi, he does not know the Rolands, but he was drinking in the bar that night when your brother was injured. He says that the brawl followed an argument between some local men and some legionnaires, during which Desirée Roland's name was mentioned, with an allusion to the mountains.'

'What did the man understand by that?'

'He made nothing of it, and did not even remember it until I questioned him. All he can recollect is that he heard the girl's name and a phrase about the mountains, then the fight started.'

'The commandant didn't mention that.'

Jean shrugged. 'He would not be told of it, nor would the police. No one would wish to get involved, you understand. This man owes me a favour, that is the only reason he consented to discuss the matter with me.'

'It doesn't really help, does it?' said Marisa blankly.

'There is one more piece of information I obtained from another source. The Rolands came originally from a village in the mountains called Sanmarina. They have lived in Calvi for many years, but when Desirée Roland left school she went back to the village to stay with an aunt and uncle and only returned to Calvi a year ago. I thought that if you were to visit the village you might be able to discover something more about her.'

'I can't imagine what,' said Marisa, 'but thank you, Jean, for all you've done. You've been very kind to take so much trouble.'

'It is nothing, *mademoiselle*. I wish it could have been more.'

Marisa went to her room and sat down on the bed. What Jean had told her brought her no nearer to solving

98

the problem of Desirée, and it seemed very unlikely that she would learn anything further if she went to this village. She mulled over the matter until finally she came to a decision. If she could get an immediate flight to England she would take it and go, but if there had to be a delay of a day or two then she would ask Leonie to lend her her car and drive out to Sanmarina. Even if it proved to be a fruitless errand it would get her away from the villa for a few hours and distract her mind from the future.

When she rang the airport the next morning she was told that there was no available flight before the weekend, four days away, so she booked a seat and then told Leonie of her impending departure.

'Oh, don't go,' urged Leonie. 'We'll all miss you.'

'You don't really need me now that your husband's here,' pointed out Marisa. 'He looks after Fiona so well that there's nothing left for me to do for her.'

'If you must go I suppose you must,' sighed Leonie. She added shrewdly: 'I imagine you've come to this sudden decision because of this Roland girl turning up here at the villa.'

'Yes,' admitted Marisa. 'I know Giselle doesn't like it and I can't blame her for that. I'm going back to England so that I can put Desirée Roland right out of my mind. I know it's the most sensible thing to do, but my conscience isn't clear about it because I still can't make up my mind whether or not I ought to help her.' She hesitated and then plunged on: 'I've heard that up to a year ago she was living with an aunt and uncle in a village in the mountains not too far from here, so I wondered if I could borrow your car to go up there and see if I could learn any more about her. If I can't then that's that, but I think I ought to make the effort.'

'You can certainly borrow the car, but are you sure you want to drive along those mountain roads?' asked Leonie doubtfully.

'Oh yes, I shall be all right as long as I drive carefully.'

99

'Then you can have the car the day after tomorrow.'

'Thank you very much. I thought I wouldn't mention to Fiona that I was leaving until the day before I go.'

'No, better, not, because she'll probably be upset. Fortunately Jon will be here to comfort her.'

Marisa announced her intended departure that evening at dinner. Jon received the news with genuine regret, Giselle with false sympathy and Blake with no visible sign of emotion, though he did say: 'I understood you were staying until the end of the summer.'

'Well, it's not exactly lively for Marisa here,' pointed out Giselle. 'She is the odd one out, isn't she?'

It was a warm evening with a full moon, and Marisa felt disinclined for sleep. Having said good night, instead of going up to her room she wandered out into the garden and sat down on the white-painted seat under the acacia tree. She would miss the fragrance and the warmth of Corsica, and she fell into a kind of half-dream of what might have happened if Giselle had never come to stay at the villa. It was wishful thinking, she knew, but it softened the hard edge of reality a little, and she was roused from it so abruptly that she blinked at the man standing before her.

'Rather a sudden decision to go home, isn't it?' stated Blake.

'Not really. I ought to have gone before when I couldn't make up my mind what to do about the relationship between Desirée Roland and Michael. All I did was postpone the inevitable conclusion, and I can't shilly-shally any longer.'

'Don't sound so contemptuous about yourself,' he said mildly. 'It isn't a crime not to be able to make up your mind immediately over something.'

'It is when other people have to suffer from your vacillation. Desirée Roland is trying to force my hand by hanging round the villa and making a nuisance of herself. The only way I can put a stop to that is by going home.'

'Thereby dooming yourself for ever to a feeling of

guilt because you didn't help her when perhaps you ought to have done.'

'You're right, of course, which is why I'm making one final effort to be fair. Jean has been pursuing some enquiries about her for me and I've decided to pay a visit to this village where she lived for some time.'

Marisa went on to tell Blake what Jean's friend had heard in the bar, ending: 'So Leonie is going to lend me her car and I'll drive myself up into the mountains and hope that luck will be with me.'

'You'll do no such thing,' said Blake decisively.

Marisa stared at him. 'Certainly I shall.'

'With no experience at all of driving on those mountain roads?'

'I can't come to any harm if I'm careful,' argued Marisa. 'I shan't take any risks.'

'And what about if you meet someone else who is taking risks? If you're set on undertaking this journey then I'll drive you to Sanmarina.'

'But there's no need for that. Truly I shall be all right.'

Even as she spoke Marisa wanted nothing so much as to be overruled. To be alone with Blake in the close proximity of a car for a whole day would be mingled agony and ecstasy, but she would willingly endure the pain for the sake of the pleasure.

'You're not driving up there alone and that's flat. We shall have to go tomorrow, though, because I can't manage the next day.'

'That will suit me just as well,' said Marisa meekly.

'Then if I'm to be away all day tomorrow I'll go and finish the work I've started. Good night.'

Marisa went to tell Leonie that she wouldn't be needing her car after all, and then up to her room to stand by her window staring out over the moonlit garden. Tomorrow would probably be the last time she would be alone with Blake, for once she had left the island they weren't likely to meet again. She tried to concentrate on plans for the future, but it was impossible. All she could think about was the next day- and Blake.

She slept very badly and was up early, creeping down to make her own breakfast and then finding to her surprise that Blake was already in the kitchen.

'Hallo,' he said, 'you've timed it nicely. Suzanne has just brought the croissants from the bakery.'

Suzanne was the daily help who came on her bicycle from a village five miles away and who now entered beaming with a wicker basket of croissants.

'Shall I make the coffee?' offered Marisa.

'No need, it's ready,' and Blake poured out a fragrant cupful, passing Marisa a yellow jug of hot milk.

'You're a man of many talents,' she said laughingly, and he grinned back at her.

'My culinary skill is limited, I'm afraid. Omelettes and coffee are about all I can manage.'

When they had finished eating he suggested they made a start.

'We don't want to rush along; we might as well take things easily.'

Marisa wondered whether he had mentioned the expedition to Giselle and if not whether he was anxious to get away before she should come down. Then she closed her mind to all speculation. This was to be a last day of enchantment, and even if it didn't solve the problem of Desirée Roland she intended to enjoy it to the full.

The road up into the mountains was narrow and twisted like a corkscrew, but Blake drove with care and skill so that Marisa lost all apprehension in spite of the steep drop. Streams trickled down the rocky slopes, and they passed fountains made of cobblestones where the water collected in a trough. Marisa exclaimed at the number of old cars, stripped of all useful parts, which were rusting in the laybys or had been tipped over the precipice to lie tangled in the bushes half way down the slopes.

102

'Yes, they are an eyesore,' agreed Blake, 'but I suppose when they break down in awkward situations the effort of getting them back to civilisation isn't worth it. What do you think of the roadside tombs?'

'Fascinating. They're exactly like miniature houses standing in their own little plots. That one we've just passed had a plate over the grilled door which said: "Famille Giovanni Valenti." '

'Some of the tombs in the cemeteries are very elaborate with wreaths of artificial flowers attached to the top.'

The village was perched on a crag, the houses clinging to the cliff face. Blake parked the car in the village square which had a fountain in the centre of it opposite to the church. Swallows were wheeling round the bell tower, but there was no other sign of life.

'What do we do now?' asked Marisa.

'I think first we'll try to contact the priest. He's bound to know everyone in the village. I imagine that's the presbytery next to the church, but let's begin by looking in the church itself in case he's there.'

They pushed open the heavy oak door, advancing into a dimness smelling of wax, incense, and crumbling stone. As they walked quietly towards the altar a side door opened and a man in a shabby cassock appeared. He glanced at them, and Blake moved forward, saying: 'Father, we hope you can help us.'

'Certainly, if it is possible,' he answered, and Blake told him that they were looking for any members of a family named Roland who had lived there some years ago. He described Desirée and mentioned that it was only a year since she had returned to Calvi.

The priest shook his head. 'I have been here only six months, so would not remember the young woman. However, there is a Madame Roland, a widow, who lives in a house at the bottom of the main street, and she may be some connection.'

Blake thanked him and he and Marisa left the church to make their way down the narrow, steeply sloping street. There was a group of shabby peeling cottages, and outside the end one stood a middle-aged woman in a navy print dress and striped apron with a kerchief over her head. In spite of the warmth of the day she wore black woollen stockings and heavy shoes, staring after them as they walked past her. Below her cottage the road deteriorated into a stony track, and Marisa murmured: 'Do you suppose she's the Madame Roland the priest was talking about?'

'I think she must be,' answered Blake. 'At any rate, she's the only other person we've seen, so we might as well approach her.'

They turned round and she watched them walk towards her, still staring.

'Madame Roland?' queried Blake, and then as she nodded he went on in French: 'Would it be possible for us to speak to you? It concerns your niece, Desirée Roland, who lives in Calvi.'

Madame burst into a torrent of speech, and made signs that they were to enter the cottage, so they stepped into a room which was rather dark and full of heavy, old-fashioned furniture. Marisa perched on the end of an ancient sofa while Blake sat down in a wooden armchair, and all the time Madame Roland was talking and gesticulating. Her accent was so thick that Marisa could make out very little of what she was saying, but it was enough to gather that there was no affection between herself and Desirée. Blake was listening intently, and when Madame paused for breath he turned to Marisa.

'Did you get all that? Desirée did live with her, but she utterly repudiates her now.'

'I grasped that, but why?'

'Apparently Desirée did something for which her aunt can never forgive her.'

'Something criminal?'

'I don't think so.'

As they spoke Madame's eyes were darting from one to the other, but it was obvious that she didn't understand

English at all, so Marisa leaned forward and said slowly in French: 'Madame, I am interested in your niece because she was going to marry my brother who is now dead.'

This had an electric effect on Madame Roland. She gave a cry and threw her hands up to heaven, then burst out: 'But that is impossible' She is already married.'

'Married?' echoed Marisa in stupefaction. 'Are you sure? Do please explain.'

Now that she had grasped the situation Madame Roland was only too willing to go into detail. Marisa was informed that Desirée's father was Madame Roland's brother-in-law and when Desirée was quite small he had decided to forsake the village life in favour of the town. However, he had not prospered there from Madame Roland's scornful expression Marisa gathered that she considered her brother-in-law to be an idle good-for-nothing and hampered by his wife's failing health they had lived a hand-to-mouth existence When Desirée left school Madame Roland and her husband, who had no children of their own, invited her to stay with them for a while and help on the smallholding which they cultivated, so she came back to live in the village.

Not long afterwards Monsieur Roland died and his widow sold the smallholding and retired to this cottage. There was talk of Desirée returning to Calvi, but a neighbour, a middle-aged widower with a prosperous farm, having taken a fancy to the girl proposed marriage. Madame Roland pointed out to her niece that it was a splendid opportunity for her since she had no dowry, so Desirée accepted him and after the wedding went to live on the farm. However, it was not long before she began to complain of boredom, and far from helping her husband on the farm she lay in bed half the morning and then refused to cook, wash or run the house properly.

She became friendly with a mechanic at the garage in the next village, and he gave her lifts into Calvi on the back of his motorbike. Finally she disappeared one afternoon, staying away until the next morning, and when her

105

husband upbraided her she flounced out of the house, taking various items of jewellery which had belonged to his first wife and all the money she could lay her hands on.

'Antoine was too good to her,' declared Madame Roland dramatically. 'He was a saint, that one. He refused to call in the police but said only that he did not wish to see her again. I can never forgive her. She brought shame upon the name of Roland in this village where it has been respected for so many years.'

'And her husband is still alive, *madame*?' queried Blake.

'*Mais certainement*. You may go to see him if you wish. His farm is only a few kilometres from here.'

'That won't be necessary. Thank you, *madame*, for being so helpful.'

'I'm very grateful to you, *madame*. You've solved a problem for me,' added Marisa.

They said goodbye and walked through the village to the car.

'To think that Desirée was married all the time,' commented Marisa. 'That was something I never expected.'

'Neither did I,' agreed Blake, 'but it's easy to see how your brother became involved in a fight over her. Obviously someone made some derogatory allusion to Desirée's past, perhaps jeered at Michael for not being aware she was married, and he jumped up to defend her.'

'And all the time she wasn't worth it,' said Marisa bitterly. 'If it hadn't been for her he might have been alive today.'

'Try not to dwell on it too much,' responded Blake gently. 'We could be mistaken. The fight might have been caused by something else.'

'But you don't believe that and neither do I.' Marisa blinked back the tears determinedly. 'Still, I agree it does no good to brood over it, and I'm very grateful to you for driving me here today and at least showing me that I owe Desirée Roland nothing at all.'

'So you can forget her completely and go back to England with a clear conscience. Now let's find a picnic spot off the road and eat our lunch.'

They drove on until they came to a cleft in the rocks and a path which led up the hillside.

'That looks promising,' said Blake. 'We'll drive on to the next layby, which shouldn't be far away, and then walk back.'

They were able to park the car a short distance further on, then carrying the picnic bag they scrambled up the hillside until they came to a natural grassy hollow sheltered by a clump of bushes. Here they sat down in the shade of a rock and unpacked the picnic basket which contained crisp buttered rolls chicken legs, tomatoes, peaches and petits fours. Blake had included a bottle of white wine in an insulated bag and there was a flask of coffee.

'This is luxury,' commented Marisa, and when they had both eaten heartily she lay back on the springy turf and reflected sleepily that this was a perfect interlude, something she would remember for the rest of her life.

She must have dozed off because she came back to consciousness to realise that some time had elapsed since she was now lying in the full sun. She raised herself on one elbow and discovered that Blake was also stretched out a few yards away, his eyes closed. She decided that she had better repack the picnic basket, so trying not to make a noise she began to gather the various bits and pieces together. The flask which had held the coffee was on the far side of him, so she leaned across to reach for it, overbalanced and landed on top of him. He gave a groan, opened his eyes, and before she could scramble away held her to him with one arm and kissed her thoroughly.

To say that Marisa was surprised was an understatement. The fall had knocked most of the breath out of her and Blake's kiss deprived her of what was left. When his arm fell away she could only gasp at first and then stammer: 'I—I didn't mean to give you such a rude awakening.'

'Didn't you?' he said with maddening calm. 'I thought

you did it to attract my attention.'

'Of course I didn't, it was an accident. Was that why you kissed me?' demanded Marisa in a rush.

Blake grinned at her. 'Not entirely.'

It was as if her bones turned to jelly and she had to force herself to get up, afraid of what might happen if she remained beside him staring at him. If he could ignore the fact temporarily that he was going to marry Giselle Marisa couldn't afford to. That kiss had affected her profoundly, and if she weren't to be involved in further heartbreak she would have to keep a tight hold on herself. Only it was so hard to do it. She loved Blake, she was afraid she would always love him, and every instinct prompted her to pour out that love without thinking of the consequences.

Resolutely she finished packing the picnic basket and then faced him.

'I think we ought to be starting back. We don't want to be late for dinner.'

'It isn't a desperate crime if we are. As a matter of fact, I thought we might stop at a small hotel I know of, quite out in the wilds, and have dinner there.'

Marisa knew she ought to be firm and say that she would prefer to return to the villa. What was the point of dragging things out when she was going back to England in three more days? No point at all, but in spite of that she was going to do it; she couldn't help herself.

So she smiled back at him and said: 'It's an attractive idea.'

'It's an even more attractive place,' he told her as they settled themselves in the car. 'I discovered it when I was exploring the island last year, and I made up my mind to revisit it at the first opportunity. I'm keeping my fingers crossed that it hasn't been enlarged or spoilt in any way.'

It was as if nothing could go wrong. They left the mountain road and struck inland until they came to a tiny village with a gravel square shaded by trees and the inevitable fountain. The hotel was a long, low building set in a semi-wild garden through which flowed a tiny stream. A rough wooden table and chairs were set out under the trees, and the proprietor carried out their aperitifs himself.

'It's a family concern,' explained Blake. 'His wife does the cooking and his daughter waits on table. The service is rather casual and sometimes the interval between courses is a bit prolonged, but what does that matter?'

'What indeed?' echoed Marisa dreamily, sipping her deliciously cold Suze. 'This is a perfect place.'

'I'm glad you like it. I thought you might.'

They went into the dining-room with its heavy beams and cool tiled floor. The tables were covered with coarse snowy cloths which smelt as if they had been dried on the rosemary bushes that dotted the garden, and there was a posy of wild flowers on the table. They ate a home-made soup thick with fresh vegetables, *côte de veau* with a salad, and finished with a lemon sorbet, drinking a pleasant local red wine and asking for their coffee and cognac to be served outside under the trees.

The minutes went by far too quickly for Marisa. She and Blake seemed completely attuned, and she listened enthralled as he described his adventures in Europe where he had spent a year after leaving university ambling slowly from capital to capital studying various forms of architecture.

'For that I had to thank my grandfather,' he said. 'He left a sum of money in trust for me until I was twenty-one, and I decided to use it to finance the trip. My father didn't really agree with what I proposed to do, but he was a reasonable man and thought I ought to be able to please myself. As a result I spent an unforgettable year, just at the right age to appreciate all I was seeing, and I've never regretted it.'

'It sounds a wonderful experience. Tell me more; what was Sweden like? I've always wanted to go there.'

Blake obliged with a graphic description of Stockholm, of cruising up the Gotha canal, of the still lakes and the vast pine forests. When he finally looked at his watch he said ruefully: 'You shouldn't be such a good listener. You've made me forget the time completely, but now we shall have to be heading for home or Leonie and Jon will be sending out a search party.'

The sun was setting in the sea when they reached the coast road and flooding the sky with gold. Both of them were rather silent, and when they reached the villa Blake halted the car to look at Marisa consideringly.

'Tired?' he queried, and she shook her head.

'No. Thank you for today. It's been heavenly.'

'It isn't over yet,' he began, and then the front door of the villa was flung open and Giselle came running down the steps.

'Blake,' she cried, 'where have you been? I've almost gone out of my mind waiting for you! I had a cable a couple of hours ago. Daddy's suffered a heart attack and he's very ill. I rang the airport and managed to get two cancellations on an early morning flight to Gatwick. You'll come with me, won't you? I can't travel alone.'

Blake got out of the car and put his arm round her shoulders.

'Yes, I'll come with you. Tell me exactly what the cable said,'—and they went into the villa together.

Marisa, left in the car, opened the passenger door and slowly got out. Her lovely day had come to an abrupt end and perhaps it was just as well. Now there was no longer any room for doubt. She had been shown quite clearly that Giselle came first in Blake's life and always would.

CHAPTER VII

Marisa was met by Leonie, who looked harassed.

'Thank goodness you're back,' she said. 'Perhaps Blake will be able to persuade Giselle to lie down for a couple of hours before they start for the airport. If she doesn't she'll be worn out by the time they reach London.'

'When did the cable arrive?'

'Just as Marie was about to serve dinner,' said Leonie ruefully, 'and naturally as a result none of us has had anything to eat, which doesn't help matters. Added to that Fiona's been playing up and refusing to settle. I couldn't do anything with her and Jon was fully occupied with Giselle, so she's probably cried herself to sleep now.'

'I'll go and make sure she's all right,' said Marisa, and ran up the stairs.

She tiptoed into the little girl's bedroom and saw that Fiona was asleep, her hair a tangled mass and her cheeks flushed. As Marisa bent over her she moved restlessly and opened her eyes.

'I'm thirsty,' she complained. 'Can I have a drink of lemonade?'

'Yes,' promised Marisa. 'Lie still and I'll go and fetch it.'

She went down to the kitchen and filled a glass from the jug of lemonade in the fridge. Fiona took it from her and drained it, then demanded: 'Some more, please.'

'Not tonight,' said Marisa. 'Look, I'm going to sponge your hands and face, then I'll comb your hair and turn your pillow. Now, isn't that more comfortable?'

'Yes.' Fiona lay down and said drowsily: 'Don't go away, stay here with me and tell me a story.'

'Very well.' Marisa sat down by the bed and began a story in her most soothing voice. Long before it was finished Fiona had fallen asleep, and after covering her with a sheet Marisa crept out of the room.

'She's fast asleep,' reported Marisa to Leonie, who said: 'Thank goodness. I've urged Giselle to rest, but she says she can't.'

'Shall I go and make some coffee?' suggested Marisa. 'It might help matters.'

'Yes, I expect Blake would be glad of some. He can't very well disappear to snatch an hour's rest if Giselle won't.'

To Marisa's relief there was no sign of Marie in the kitchen, so presumably she and Jean had retired to their own quarters. The girl saw a pan of soup at the side of the stove, so she heated it while the coffee was percolating and cut sandwiches. Leonie and Jon must be hungry by now and Blake might be able to persuade Giselle to take a little soup.

When Marisa appeared with a loaded trolley Giselle was sitting on the sofa with her hand in Blake's. Her lovely eyes were swollen and she was very pale, but she seemed reasonably calm now. With a mixture of firmness and gentleness he coaxed her to take some soup and then to stretch out on the sofa.

'I couldn't sleep,' declared Giselle wildly. 'You couldn't expect me to.'

'I don't,' answered Blake calmly, 'but if you just close your eyes and relax you'll be in much better shape to endure the plane journey and to see your father when you reach London.'

Obediently Giselle lay back and closed her eyes.

'Don't leave me,' she murmured, and Blake took her hand again, saying: 'I won't.'

He looked at Marisa. 'Why don't you go to bed, Marisa? You can't do anything by staying up, and you'll have Fiona to cope with in the morning.'

She felt as if she were being banished, but knew that what he said was true and with a quiet good night she pushed the trolley into the kitchen to wash up the cups and plates. A kind of numbness spread over her. She realised it was quite possible that she was seeing Blake for the last time, but somehow she couldn't take it in properly. She crept up the stairs and lay in bed listening until eventually she heard the sound of a car engine and knew that he and Giselle were setting off for the airport. It was a dreadful situation for Giselle, but in spite of that Marisa envied her. Naturally she was racked with anxiety, but she had Blake to comfort her, and his support would have made any ordeal endurable to Marisa.

Everyone was in low spirits in the morning, even Jon's good humour was dimmed. Fiona was fractious and heavy-eyed, refusing her breakfast and complaining that she felt sick.

'I think she had too much sun yesterday,' said Leonie. 'She'd better play quiet in the shade today. Oh dear, it's going to be dull without both Giselle and Blake; I must give Roger a ring. By the way, how did you get on with your quest yesterday? Was it successful?'

'I'd forgotten all about it,' confessed Marisa. 'Yes, it was very successful and removed any doubts I might have had about misjudging Desirée. She couldn't have married Michael, because she was married all the time and still is.'

'Married? To whom?'

Marisa related the story and said: 'I was very glad to have my mind made up once and for all, and I shouldn't have managed it if it hadn't been for Blake. Madame Roland would never have responded to me as she did to him.'

'Yes, he has his faults, but he does provide a good shoulder to lean on. He's left his car behind for us to use. He and Giselle went to Bastia in her hired car and arranged to leave it at the airport.'

The day dragged on. Roger rolled up in the afternoon and Leonie greeted him with cries of joy.

'Oh, how thankful I am to see you; I'm so dreadfully bored. What have you been doing with yourself? It seems ages since you were here.'

'A spot of honest toil,' said Roger. 'In other words a
113

crash course in English for a man who wants to do business with an English firm. I thought we'd all go out to dinner to celebrate my unusual affluence.'

'Lovely,' said Leonie. 'It's just what I need.'

'Right,' replied Roger.

He spent a couple of hours lazing by the pool and then left, saying he would be back around seven.

'Thank goodness for someone cheerful,' said Leonie. 'Fiona, what is the matter with you? You've been grizzling all day.'

'My tummy feels funny,' wailed Fiona.

'Then you'd better go inside and lie down.'

'Don't want to lie down.'

'Then what do you want?' demanded her mother in exasperation.

'Don't know,' and Fiona burst into loud sobs.

Jon had taken Blake's car into Calvi after lunch to have a slight fault rectified and he now appeared.

'What's the matter?' he enquired, regarding his weeping daughter.

'Heaven knows,' retorted Leonie crossly. 'She's been the picture of misery all day. I think an early bedtime's indicated. By the way, Jon, Roger called and he wants us all to dine with him tonight at that hotel on the coast. I'll ask Marie to baby-sit.'

'Oh, all right. I'm not much in the mood for it myself, but if you want to go—'

'I do,' said Leonie crisply. 'I can hardly wait to get into a more lively atmosphere.'

'Come along, sweetheart, I'll carry you up to bed and Marisa shall bring you your supper,' said Jon, picking up his daughter while Marisa went into the kitchen to collect the little girl's supper tray.

When she carried it into the bedroom Fiona was lying back on her pillows with her eyes closed while her father was regarding her perplexedly.

'Do you think there's anything the matter with her?' he asked Marisa. 'She's not usually so fretful.'

114

'I wondered that myself,' answered Marisa, 'but I'm not familiar with children's illnesses. Could she be sickening for measles or something like that?'

'I suppose so,' said Jon helplessly, 'but apart from getting hold of a doctor I don't know who to consult. Marie has no children and Leonie's as ignorant as we are.'

'I think it's a little early to call a doctor,' ventured Marisa. 'As Leonie said, it may be just a touch of the sun and Fiona will be better in the morning.'

'Yes, you're probably right,' agreed Jon with relief. 'Well, I must get changed to leave the field clear for Leonie.'

When he had gone Marisa tried to coax Fiona to eat her supper, but the little girl shook her head.

'Don't want it. I feel sick,' and the next moment she had vomited all over the sheets.

She began to wail again, and Marisa said: 'Oh, poor baby! Lie still, darling, just for a moment, and I'll soon have you cleaned up.'

She ran out of the room to the linen chest on the landing as Leonie reached the head of the stairs.

'What's the matter?' asked Leonie as Marisa opened the chest and began to take out clean sheets.

'Fiona's been sick. I'm afraid she really isn't well.'

'She's probably been eating a lot of rubbish, and she'll feel better now. I suspect Jean of giving her sweets, but I've never been able to catch him at it. Can you cope?'

'Yes, I can cope,' said Marisa dryly, and went back to Fiona.

In a short time the little girl had been sponged and settled back into bed again. She seemed drowsy, but Marisa made up her mind not to leave her. She had no desire to dine at the hotel tonight, and this would be a good excuse for her to stay behind.

When Leonie came into the room in a glamorous outfit of apricot wild silk Marisa said: 'I'm not coming to

115

the hotel. I'd rather stay with Fiona in case she should be sick again.'

'Nonsense, she'll be all right now,' insisted Leonie in some annoyance. 'Marie will look after her.'

Marisa shook her head. 'I'd rather stay. I shouldn't enjoy myself if I went out.'

'What's the matter?' asked Jon, coming into the room in his turn.

Marisa explained, and he looked uneasy. 'If Fiona's not well I don't think we should leave the responsibility of her to Marie. I'll stay behind too.'

'You're both being ridiculous,' cried Leonie. 'She's simply suffering from an overdose of ice cream or sweets, and she'll have recovered by morning. Make martyrs of yourselves if you want to, but I shall go with Roger.'

Her lovely face was flushed with temper, and as Roger's car drew up at this moment she ran downstairs to greet him at the door. A moment later there was the sound of a car door slamming and then of its engine bursting into life as it roared down the drive.

Jon looked ruefully at Marisa. 'I expect Leonie's right and we are a pair of fools. Still, I'd rather be——'

'Safe than sorry,' completed Marisa. 'Fiona's asleep now, so we might as well go downstairs. I'll leave the sitting-room door open so that we can hear her if she calls.'

'And I'll go and tell Marie that her services won't be needed.'

It was a warm night, so they settled themselves by the open french windows.

Jon said apologetically: 'Leonie isn't really as heartless as she sounds, you know. It's chiefly my fault. I persuaded her to marry me before she was ready to settle down, and then Fiona was born in the first year, curtailing her freedom still further.'

'I think Leonie will enjoy Fiona when she's older and they have more in common,' said Marisa tactfully.

Privately she thought that Leonie was both selfish and

116

spoilt and that Jon gave in to her far too readily. It wasn't surprising since he adored her; it was easy to see that. The trouble was that he adored Fiona too, and was constantly pulled first one way and the other between the conflicting claims of both his wife and his daughter.

'What about something to eat?' suggested Marisa. 'Shall I go and forage?'

'Could you?' Anything will do. I didn't dare suggest Marie should prepare something after Leonie had told her we would all be dining out.'

Marisa was crossing the hall when she heard a wail from upstairs followed by a shriek of pain. She sped up the stairs, calling: 'I'm coming, darling, I'm coming,' and ran into the bedroom to find that Fiona had been sick again and was now writhing in agony, her screams echoing through the house. Jon was there almost as quickly, and as he bent to pick up his little daughter she shuddered in his arms, moaning: 'Take the pain away, Daddy, take it away!'

'I will, darling, I will, just as soon as I can.' His eyes met Marisa's and she said: 'I think it must be appendicitis.'

'I'll ring the doctor.'

In a few moments he was back again to say that Doctor Monet was coming immediately, and then the two of them tried to soothe Fiona. Fortunately the doctor was as good as his word, and after a brief examination confirmed Marisa's diagnosis, adding that the appendix had probably perforated.

'It will be necessary for the child to come into a nursing home in Ile-Rousse,' he said, 'and in order that there should be the least possible delay we will wrap her up warmly and take her there in my car.'

Jon swathed Fiona in blankets and carried her down to the car while Marisa packed a few necessities in a case, then joined him. Between them they supported Fiona as the doctor drove to Ile-Rousse and then they surrendered her to the care of the nuns at the nursing home, being shown into a small room to wait. Jon's face was haggard, and Marisa felt intensely sorry for him.

'Hadn't we better ring the hotel and tell Leonie what's happened?' she suggested. 'We might be here some time, and we can't let her go back to the villa unsuspecting.'

'No, of course not. I'll ring her now.'

Jon disappeared to find a telephone while Marisa sat there praying that Fiona was in less pain, that they had managed to get here in time. Jon came back to say that Roger was driving Leonie to the nursing home immediately, and the two of them arrived in about half an hour. Leonie was completely distraught, her volatile nature precipitating her into an extreme of remorse for leaving Fiona at all.

'I didn't think she was really ill,' she said distractedly, 'just a little out of sorts. Oh, Jon, appendicitis isn't really serious these days, is it, only of course there's always the danger of peritonitis.'

'Dr. Monet said he hoped they'd caught it in time. They're operating now.'

'Oh, Jon!'

He put his arms round her and eased her into a chair. Roger coughed uneasily.

'Is there anything I can do?' he asked. 'Anything at all?'

'There's no point in us all staying here,' answered Jon, 'so I'd be grateful if you'd run Marisa back to the villa.'

'Willingly,' said Roger with alacrity.

Realising that she was serving no useful purpose by sitting at the nursing home, Marisa made no protest but said: 'I shall be waiting up,' and then: 'I'm ready, Roger.'

He took her arm as they walked to the car.

'Am I thankful to get out of that place,' he said. 'I loathe hospitals.'

'I don't think anyone enjoys them,' said Marisa dryly.

'Poor little Fiona, still, kids are very resilient. She'll probably be rushing round the place in no time. Funny, I never thought Leonie would go to pieces like that; she doesn't strike me as the maternal type.'

Roger chatted lightheartedly as he drove to the villa, and Marisa felt confirmed in her previous judgement that he was charming but superficial. Nothing which didn't interfere with his own comfort would ever affect him deeply. She said good night to him and then let herself into the villa where she curled up on the sofa in the sitting-room. She knew she wouldn't sleep if she went to bed, so she stayed there, dreading to hear the telephone ring until just before dawn she fell into a light doze.

She was aroused from this by the sound of a key in the lock and leaped to her feet as Leonie and Jon came in. Leonie looked pale and drawn with her make-up all smudged, but she was smiling tremulously.

'The operation's been a success, Marisa,' she cried, 'but it was touch and go. The appendix had perforated and the poison was spreading through Fiona's body, poor lamb, but they caught it in time.'

'I'm so thankful,' said Marisa. 'I'll go and make some coffee. I think we all need it.'

Marie and Jean came into the kitchen as she was filling the percolator and enquired anxiously about Fiona.

'*Pauvre petite,*' exclaimed Marie, 'but the good nuns will soon make her better. When she comes home I will bake the chocolate gateau she loves so much.'

The coffee drunk, Leonie was persuaded to lie down and Marisa urged Jon to go to bed too.

'I'll be here,' she said, 'and if there should be any word from the nursing home I'll let you know immediately.'

'No, you go up to bed as well as Leonie,' said Jon. 'I don't feel much like sleep yet; I'll snatch an hour or two after lunch.' He hesitated. 'Marisa, I've been wondering if I dared ask you a favour. I know you've arranged to go back to England tomorrow, but would it be possible for you to stay on here? I must return myself in another week, but Fiona certainly won't be fit to travel and I don't want to leave Leonie to cope alone with her. If you were here I'd feel so much easier in my mind.'

119

'I could stay on,' said Marisa slowly. 'Now that this business with Desirée Roland is cleared up there isn't the same urgency for me to get away.'

'Bless you,' said Jon, and putting his arm round her he gave her a brotherly kiss. They both heard a slight sound and there was Leonie standing in the doorway.

'I forgot my bag,' she explained, and came forward to take it from a chair.

'Marisa's staying on,' volunteered Jon, 'so you won't have to look after Fiona by yourself.'

'Thank you,' said Leonie tonelessly, and ran back up the stairs.

There was a rather awkward silence, and then Jon commanded: 'Off you go; you must be dropping with fatigue.'

Marisa went up to her room feeling embarrassed. She was aware Jon had meant nothing by his casual embrace, but did Leonie realise that? Marisa contemplated tapping on her door to reassure her, but decided that it might make matters worse.

It was another twenty-four hours before Fiona was out of danger, then her temperature dropped and she began to make progress. Leonie and Jon spent every afternoon at the nursing home, and then at the end of the following week Jon flew back to England.

For the first time ever Marisa saw Leonie cling to her husband as they said goodbye.

'Couldn't you stay on a bit longer, Jon, so that we could all go home together?' she begged.

'My sweet, you know I can't,' he said firmly. 'I've already extended my leave by a couple of days and that's the utmost I can manage Anyway, Fiona's improving so rapidly that you ought to be able to follow me in about a fortnight, and in the meantime you'll have Marisa to keep you company.'

'Yes, but it isn't the same,' insisted Leonie intensely, and twined her arms round his neck.

Marisa said: 'Goodbye, Jon, have a good journey,'

and went inside to leave them alone together, busying herself in looking for a favourite storybook of Fiona's which the little girl had asked for. She herself was wondering if she had made a mistake in agreeing to stay on since she wasn't at all sure that Leonie wanted her. Jon's wife had been decidedly cool to her during the last week, and though she was essentially a creature of moods she had always been companionable and friendly towards Marisa before.

Ironically enough, now that Marisa had no need to dread her appearance there was no sign of Desirée. The girl wondered why Desirée had abandoned her blackmailing tactics, but wasn't disposed to seek her out to triumph over her; far better to forget the whole business. Therefore when Marisa drove into Calvi one afternoon while Leonie was at the nursing home she avoided passing the restaurant, so that it was only by chance that she ran into Desirée at the corner of one of the streets which lay parallel to the sea front.

'Sorry,' said Marisa automatically, then looked again.

'Oh,' she exclaimed, and Desirée tossed her head.

'There is no need to regard me like that. It is not a crime to leave one's husband, even though my aunt thinks it is. She sent a message to say that two people had called and I recognised you from her description.'

'It's a crime to contemplate marriage to another man when your husband is still alive,' countered Marisa.

'What do you know of love and passion?' sneered Desirée. 'Antoine had land and money, but he was old and dried up. He was content for every day to be like the last, but I wanted to see life and have pretty clothes. Michel promised that in England I should have everything I desired. Who there would have known that I was married to Antoine? I should never have returned to Corsica again.'

Marisa sighed. 'Whatever Michael promised you he would have found it difficult to keep his word. Even if he'd succeeded in escaping from the Legion and getting

121

back to England he would have had no job and no means of providing for you.'

'There was his rich uncle,' insisted Desirée obstinately. 'We could have lived with him for a while, but now he is dead and you will keep everything for yourself.'

'Obviously you won't believe me, but my uncle wasn't rich.'

'Why should you grudge me some of the money when you will have a man to provide for you? I saw him with you, and he cannot be poor, wearing good clothes like that.'

'I don't know what you're talking about.'

'But certainly you do. He accompanied you the second time you came to the resturant, and he looked at you in the way a man looks when he desires a woman, though to me it is quite incomprehensible he should want you. You have nothing to recommend you at all!'

Marisa stared at her. Desirée must mean Blake, and she couldn't have been more mistaken.

'You're quite wrong, and I don't think we've anything more to say to each other.'

Desirée glared and flounced away, while Marisa finished her shopping and then drove back to the villa. She was using the car Blake had hired, leaving the other free for Leonie, who was still absent when Marisa let herself in but who appeared in half an hour looking tired and wan.

'Would you like a cup of tea?' Marisa asked. 'I imagine you need one. How is Fiona?'

'Progressing very satisfactorily, and yes, I'd love a cup of tea.'

Marisa made it and carried a tray out to the table on the terrace. She poured a cup which Leonie took and drank thirstily. She was much more silent and preoccupied than she had been before Fiona's illness, even though the little girl was gaining strength and would soon be able to come home. Now she lay back and closed her eyes while Marisa watched her sympathetically.

'Why don't you rest tomorrow and I'll go to see Fiona,' she suggested. 'You could do with a break.'

'No, no.' Leonie's eyes flew open. 'I'm quite all right. Fiona's expecting me. I mustn't disappoint her.'

'Surely you could miss one day if someone else went instead.'

'I suppose I could, but I don't want to.'

Leonie paused as they heard the sound of a car, and then in a moment a voice called: 'Anyone at home?' and Roger appeared round the side of the villa.

'Hallo,' he said cheerfully. 'How are you both, and how's the invalid?'

'Much better, thank you,' answered Leonie, sitting up. 'Do you think there's any tea left, Marisa? Roger, you'd like a cup?'

'In fault of anything stronger,' he said with a grin.

'What's left in this pot is half cold,' said Marisa. 'I'll make some more.'

She picked up the tray and went back to the kitchen, returning in a few moments with a clean cup and a fresh pot of tea. To her surprise Leonie rushed past her into the villa, and she put down her tray with a questioning look at Roger.

'What's wrong?' she enquired.

'Search me,' he replied with a shrug. 'All I did was ask her if she'd like to go out tonight. I thought it would be a change for her after being cooped up here so long, and since Fiona's so much better there couldn't be any harm in it, but she treated my suggestion as if I'd invited her to indulge in some wild orgy.'

He sounded decidedly aggrieved, and Marisa said soothingly: 'I don't think Leonie's quite herself yet. This illness of Fiona's has been a tremendous shock to her, in fact, it's affected her considerably.'

'But it wasn't as if she were devoted to the child. Good lord, she always gave me the impression that she found Fiona a bit of a nuisance.'

'I think the realisation that she might have lost her

has made all the difference,' murmured Marisa.

'Obviously.' Roger looked sulky since he didn't take kindly to being thwarted, then suddenly he brightened. 'Well, if Leonie doesn't want to go gay what about you? There's nothing to keep you in.'

'I don't think I'm in the mood for it either,' said Marisa.

It was just one more proof of the shallowness of Roger's nature. He had been glad of Leonie as a lively companion, but he shied away from any deeper involvement. If she didn't want to play then he'd find someone who would; anyone amusing would do.

'Oh, if that's how you feel then there's no point in my lingering.'

He made no effort to hide his chagrin, said goodbye and was gone. Marisa sat down and poured herself another cup of tea, judging that Leonie would prefer to be alone for a while. She sat on the terrace reading a book until eventually Leonie appeared, then asked: 'Feeling better?'

'Why didn't you go with him?' burst out Leonie. 'I'm sure he asked you.'

'Yes, he did, after you'd refused him, but I didn't fancy his company either.'

'No, you'd rather have Jon, wouldn't you? Oh, I've been a fool, such a fool!'

'And still are, if you think Jon has eyes for anyone but you,' retorted Marisa evenly. 'I like him very much, but I'm not in love with him nor he with me. What's brought all this on, Leonie? Would you rather I went back to England now?'

'No, no—oh, I don't know what I do want. I'm all mixed up!'

Leonie flung herself down on the sofa and began to weep, the tears flooding her cheeks so that she was soon incoherent with sobs. Marisa let her cry until the storm had spent itself, then she went into the villa and emerged with a bottle of brandy and a glass.

124

'Drink this,' she said. 'I think you need something stronger than tea this time.'

Leonie drank it, choked and sniffed, then said: 'I feel better giving way. I daren't let Fiona see how miserable I was, so I've been bottling it up.'

'Did you really believe Jon and I were having an affair?' asked Marisa.

Leonie looked ashamed. 'Not in my heart, but I couldn't have blamed him if he had strayed. It wasn't until we sat in the nursing home together all that ghastly night that I realised how much I depended on him. He was like a rock. Even though he didn't know any more than I did whether Fiona was going to pull through he never let me see his doubts but said he was sure she would.'

She shifted restlessly. 'You see, Jon never wanted to marry anyone but me and didn't trouble to hide it, so that I was aware he'd sacrifice anything for me. It was very flattering, but after a while it bored me, and then when Fiona was born she cramped my style. Jon expected to settle down, and I didn't intend to, not at my age and with my looks. I craved excitement and he was so predictable, going to the office each day and preferring to spend most evenings quietly at home. I was determined to get away, so I jumped at the chance to come out here, then I met Roger and he was fun and I seriously thought of staying on with him.'

'But what would you have lived on? Roger can barely keep himself, let alone anyone else. And there was Fiona. Did you mean to send her back to England or keep her here with you?'

Leonie grimaced. 'I didn't think anything out very clearly. I suppose I imagined I'd be a lot more free without her. It wasn't until I thought she was dying that I realised how much I loved her and Jon too, that I couldn't bear to lose either of them.'

'There's no reason why you should.'

'No, but I saw Jon kiss you that day and all at once it
125

occurred to me that he might have become tired of my tantrums and be attracted to someone with a nicer nature. If that happened I'd be lost; I couldn't manage on my own.'

She gazed at Marisa with tragic eyes, and Marisa laughed.

'And you've been tormented all this time with the fear that Jon was only waiting for Fiona to recover to ditch you?'

'Well, something like that. It's not funny, Marisa. I've been absolutely wretched ever since he went.'

Even as she spoke Leonie's spirits rose. She patted her hair. 'I must look a fright. I'd better go and bathe my face.'

Already she was coming up on the rebound from her plunge into the depths of unhappiness. She would always be temperamental, but this time she had had a genuine fright and Marisa guessed that never again would she treat Jon in so cavalier a fashion. It looked as though some good had come out of Fiona's illness after all.

Leonie ate her dinner with appetite that evening, and announced that it was the first time for days she had felt hungry.

'I forgot to tell you, I had a letter from Blake this morning—another scrappy effort like the last one because he says he's rushed off his feet. Giselle's father is making a good recovery, but he won't be fit to take any responsibility for quite a time, so the administration of the firm will devolve on Blake. Apparently Mr. Lambert had been commissioned by one of the East African states to design a new civic building for the capital, and he should have flown out next week to survey the site. Now Blake will have to go in his place.'

'How long will Blake be out in Africa?'

'I don't think he knows exactly. Several weeks, certainly.'

So when I go back to England he'll be far away, thought Marisa. She remembered what Desirée had said,

126

and wondered if it could be possible that Blake cared for her a little. It didn't seem very likely, or why hadn't he written to her as well as Leonie?

Fiona continued to make rapid progress and was able to leave hospital at the end of the week. Now Leonie was all anxiety to get back to England, so she booked the first available plane seats. They were to drive to the airport, leaving the car there for the hire firm to collect, while Blake's car remained at the villa where it would be picked up by the same firm.

'You'll come back to Twickenham with us and stay over the weekend, won't you, Marisa?' invited Leonie. 'You must; you can't go straight from a plane journey to an empty house which hasn't been lived in for weeks.'

It certainly wasn't an attractive prospect, and Marisa was glad to accept the invitation.

'Thank you,' she said, 'but I must return to Clapham on Monday morning.'

'Whenever you like,' agreed Leonie gaily. 'I've enjoyed the summer here, but now I'm ready for a change. I'm dying to buy some new clothes and have my hair properly cut.'

'And I'm going to school,' said Fiona.

'Yes, darling, to a delightful nursery school not far away, and I shall have to see about getting another au pair. I might try a Philippino; I believe they're very good. What are your plans, Marisa?'

'Very vague,' said Marisa wryly. 'I suppose my first step must be to look for a flat and a job, then put the house in the hands of an agent.'

'Oh, I'm sure you'll soon get fixed up, you're so capable. If I can help at all let me know.'

For the next few days Marisa found that she was fully occupied in coping with all the packing and clearing up to be done since the villa was to be shut up for the winter, though Jean and Marie would remain in the kitchen premises as caretakers. On Thursday evening when everything was finished and dinner over Leonie declared that she simply must go to bed as she was utterly exhausted, so when she had left the room Marisa walked through the open french windows into the garden and down to the pool by which she had spent so many happy hours. It was all over now, the most memorable summer of her life. Would it have been better if she had never met Blake and so been spared the agony of parting from him? She couldn't decide.

As she stood there someone moved in the shadows and she saw Jean cross the gravel to pick up a book which was lying behind the white seat. He came over to her, holding it out.

'Ah, *mademoiselle*, you are feeling melancholy at saying goodbye to the villa?'

'Just a little, Jean. It's such a lovely place.'

She took the book from him, remembering the day in Calvi when she and Blake had bought it together, and Jean said comfortingly: 'But you will come here again; I know, I can feel it.'

She shook her head. 'I don't think so, Jean.'

'Yes, you will see. The island has cast its spell on you. It will never let you go.'

'Has it cast its spell on you, Jean? You once told me you came from Paris.'

'But I shall lay my bones here. I would not exchange the scent of the *maquis* for the boulevards now.'

Lucky Jean to have a choice, thought Marisa as she walked across the terrace and up to her room. She wasn't looking forward to going back to the gloomy house her uncle had left her and planning her life afresh. What kind of a job did she really want, and more to the point, what kind of work was she best fitted to do? The more she thought about it the more depressed she became, and then she took herself firmly in hand. First she must go back and search for a flat and a job, then put the house on the market. Until she reached home she could do neither, so she might as well postpone her worrying until she could take some action.

The journey to Bastia was rather trying. Fiona, still weak and inclined to be tearful, soon grew tired of travelling, demanding iced drinks, games to amuse her and frequent stops. Leonie and Marisa took it in turns to drive, and Leonie's temper grew more and more ragged, but at last the airport came in sight, whereupon Marisa breathed a great sigh of relief.

There was still the plane journey to be endured, but mercifully Fiona fell asleep, so the other two were able to doze themselves. Jon met them at Gatwick and Leonie flung herself into his arms, crying: 'Darling, it's wonderful to see you again!' while Fiona clung to him, saying: 'Daddy, Daddy, I've missed you!'

His face lit up at this welcome so that Marisa wished she could have faded tactfully away, but in a moment he turned to her and said: 'Marisa, it's good to see you again. Thank you for making the journey with Leonie. Is this all the luggage? Let's get it out to the car.'

Jon and Leonie's house was in Twickenham with a view of the river and Marisa was given a pretty room, all blue and white frilled chintz. Jon had been looked after by the daily woman while Leonie had remained in Corsica, and she had left a casseroled chicken in the oven together with an apple charlotte. After Fiona had been put to bed with a light supper the others sat drinking sherry in the drawing-room while Leonie brought herself up to date with all that had happened while she had been away.

'What's the latest news of Blake and Giselle?' she asked. 'In the last letter I had from him he said he was going out to one of these new African states, I can't remember which, and would be away several weeks.'

'Yes, he flew there yesterday. He's been working hard ever since he returned to England. I've only had a brief glimpse of him myself.'

'And Giselle?'

'She rang up to ask how Fiona was. Blake had told her what had happened, of course. She said she might call this weekend as she had some news for you.'

'That sounds exciting. Do you suppose she and Blake became engaged before he left?'

'I've no idea. You know how uncommunicative Blake is.'

'None better. Oh, there's so much to do now that I'm back I don't know how I'm ever going to fit it in.'

'Well, take it easy to begin with. You don't want to knock yourself up. Sue will be coming along on Sunday so she can help with things.'

They exchanged loving looks, and Marisa, intercepting these, decided to plead fatigue immediately after dinner and disappear. She carried out this programme and went to her room, expecting to lie awake for hours, but she was more tired than she knew and fell asleep almost at once.

In the morning the sun was shining, and it was quite warm. Fiona clamoured to go into the garden, and since her father was there to amuse her while Leonie was obviously all set to spend a pleasant hour or so ringing her many friends Marisa volunteered to do any necessary shopping. Leonie accepted gladly, told her where to go, and Marisa set off with a list. She managed to get all she wanted, then lingered for coffee in a café before starting her return journey.

Because it was so fine she walked, and she was turning into the drive when she almost bumped into Giselle leaving the house. She was carrying her gloves in her hand, and Marisa's gaze fastened on the square emerald surrounded by diamonds which glittered on the engagement finger. Giselle's eyes followed the other girl's and she smiled.

'I came to see Leonie and tell her my news,' she said.

'Congratulations,' responded Marisa numbly, 'though I suppose strictly speaking I ought to offer them to Blake.'

Giselle's eyelids flickered, then she smiled again. 'Oh, I'll accept them myself.'

'Excuse me, Leonie may be needing these things,' said

130

Marisa, and fled up the drive. It might look rude, but she couldn't endure to stand there talking to Giselle a moment longer. Now she would have to go into the house and Leonie would be full of the engagement. It wasn't to be borne. Marisa despised herself for a coward, but she knew she had to get away. The easiest course would be to go home today. There would be plenty to be done in the house where cleaning and polishing would tire her out and prevent her from thinking.

As she expected Leonie greeted her the moment she came in with: 'Did you meet Giselle? Did she tell you about her engagement?'

'Yes, I saw her ring,' and then before Leonie could enlarge on the subject Marisa went on: 'Leonie, should you mind very much if I went home this afternoon instead of Monday morning?'

'But the idea was that you would stay over the week-end.'

'Yes, I know, and I'm very grateful to you for the invitation, but I really think I'd like to start getting the house straight. Jon's here to help with Fiona, and Sue will be coming tomorrow.'

'And as a matter of fact I've been told of a suitable au pair. Mary Sinclair has a Japanese girl and she has a friend who is with a family in Wimbledon but wants to come to Twickenham so that they can be near each other.'

'I'm so glad for your sake.'

'She won't be like you, I'm afraid. We have enjoyed your company, Marisa, and I don't intend that we shall lose touch. It's Fiona's birthday a fortnight on Friday, and I've promised she shall have a small party. You will come to it, won't you?'

'Yes, of course I'll come,' said Marisa, and then she went to pack her case.

Fiona wept when she said goodbye, but Marisa knew that the little girl would soon forget her. Once the birthday party was over it wasn't likely they would come into contact again, and a chapter of her life would close. She tried to erase Blake's image completely from her mind and heart as she left the house in a taxi, knowing that if she didn't she must surely burst into tears.

CHAPTER VIII

Once she had reached home again Marisa gave herself no time to brood. As she had surmised, there was plenty to be done in the house, and she set to work dusting, polishing and washing paintwork until every surface was as shining as she could make it. At the same time she made enquiries about accommodation to rent, but to find a small unfurnished flat was apparently seeking the impossible, and she faced another setback when she contacted an estate agent about the sale of the house.

He shook his head depressingly after he had inspected it.

'This is a bad time to sell,' he said, 'and it's the wrong type of property—too old and too big for most people. Still, we'll put it on the books and I'll let you know how we go on.'

On Fiona's birthday Marisa made her way to Twickenham, taking with her as a present a fascinating rag doll with long golden plaits. Fiona, wildly excited and completely recovered, was pleased to see her and accepted the doll with enthusiasm. The noise was deafening. It sounded as if there were fifty children present instead of half a dozen, and Marisa noticed a tall dark girl whom she recognised as Sue supervising them in Musical Chairs. Leonie beckoned to her sister, who left the game and sauntered across to Marisa.

'Hallo,' she said. 'I never had a chance to thank you for

taking my place.'

'Not at all. I did myself a good turn. I wanted to visit Calvi, so I was able to combine business with pleasure and spend some weeks in the sun.'

'Leonie told me about your brother. I'm sorry.'

'Thank you.'

'What are you going to do now?' asked Sue. 'Have you got a job lined up?'

'Not yet. I'm looking for one and somewhere to live when I sell my house.'

Sue hesitated, then went on: 'Did Leonie tell you that I was working in a boutique and living in the flat over it? Well, Martin and I are getting married next week, just a register office affair, and joining two other couples who are setting off to travel overland to Australia in a converted bus. That was what we quarrelled about in the beginning. He wanted to leave me behind and I wasn't having it. In the end he gave way, and we've both been saving hard all summer, so now we've enough cash to make a start. The point I'm getting at is that I'll be leaving my job and the flat, and it struck me that you might like to take my place for a while.'

'I'd love to,' said Marisa, 'but I haven't had any experience of working in a boutique.'

'Nothing to it,' declared Sue airily. 'Just take an interest in people and you can't go wrong. No, seriously, I could introduce you to Sally Fairfax, the owner, and I'm sure she'd be glad to give you a trial. I know she hasn't taken on anyone else yet. Let's see what Leonie thinks.'

Sue called her sister over and put the proposition to her. Leonie approved, so it was arranged that Marisa should call in at the boutique on Monday to meet the owner. Then Sue announced that she would give Shansi a hand with the children and plunged into the mêlée again.

'Let them cope for a while,' said Leonie. 'They're younger than I am and more resilient.'

'Is Shansi satisfactory?' asked Marisa, looking across at the tiny Japanese girl with her silky black hair.

133

'Very, I'm glad to say. She has several younger brothers and sisters, so she and Fiona get on well together.'

Leonie paused and they heard the front door bell ring followed by Shansi's rather shrill voice greeting someone.

'Who can that be?' queried Leonie, getting to her feet, and the next moment the door opened and there stood Blake.

'Blake!' shrieked his sister-in-law. 'I thought you were in darkest Africa.'

'I was yesterday morning,' he said, and then Fiona grabbed his hand, crying: 'It's my birthday, Uncle Blake. Did you bring me a present?'

'Of course,' he told her. 'Happy birthday, chicken. Your present's in the hall. A square box.'

Fiona rushed out, followed by her guests, and Leonie said: 'Hadn't you noticed that Marisa was here?'

'I had.' Blake surveyed her coolly. 'How are you, Marisa?'

'Very well, thank you,' she answered sedately. 'Did you have a good flight?'

'Rather bumpy as usual.'

Fiona dashed back into the drawing-room with her present in her arms. It was half a dozen beautifully carved animals, and she crooned over them in delight.

'Blake, they're far too good for her to play with,' protested Leonie, and he answered: 'Nonsense, they'll help her feeling for line.'

By now the other children were playing with the animals too, and Leonie said rather helplessly: 'Shansi, I don't want them all in here. Isn't it time for them to have tea?'

'If you wish, Missis Wantage.'

Shansi began to shepherd the children out, and Blake turned to Marisa.

'Marisa, I——' but before he could finish Fiona darted back and began to pull him towards the door.

'Uncle Blake, you must come and watch me blow the candles out and cut the cake.'

'Are you home for good, Blake?' asked Leonie as they all trooped into the dining-room. 'I thought you expected to be abroad for several weeks.'

'This is only a flying visit. I'm going back in a couple of days, but something had cropped up which I needed to discuss with Giselle, then knowing it was Fiona's birthday I wanted to have a look at her too.'

At the mention of Giselle's name Marisa's heart gave a sickening lurch, and to disguise it she affected to be absorbed in Fiona's cutting of the cake. She joined in the chorus of 'Happy birthday to you', helping the small guests to hot sausages, pinwheel sandwiches, gingerbread men and all the other delicacies which they devoured as if they hadn't seen food for a week. She carefully avoided Blake as much as possible, which wasn't difficult since Fiona monopolised him, until the first of the mothers arrived to collect her offspring and gradually the house became calm again.

'I don't know about you, Marisa, but I'm exhausted,' sighed Leonie. 'Jon will be home very soon, so let's all have a quiet drink while Shansi puts Fiona to bed.'

'I want Uncle Blake to put me to bed,' wailed Fiona, who was overtired and ready now to dissolve into tears.

'And I must go,' said Marisa quickly.

'Not yet,' urged Leonie. 'Wait until Jon comes in and then Blake will run you home.'

It was the last thing Marisa wanted. The sight of Blake had warned her that all her efforts to forget him had been in vain. She was as much in love with him as ever, and it would be torture to sit beside him in the car making polite conversation.

As Leonie left the room with Sue and Fiona Blake remarked: 'I'd like to drive you home, Marisa, because I want to talk to you. There are things to be cleared up between us.'

Immediately she said brightly: 'Oh, I don't see any necessity for explanations. I enjoyed Corsica, but it was no more than a pleasant interlude, was it?'

His eyes narrowed. 'Was that how you saw it?'

'Of course. Didn't you?'

'In that case I agree there's nothing more to be said,' he responded evenly.

'Nothing at all.' Marisa's head was held high. 'Goodbye, Blake.'

'Goodbye, Marisa.'

She made her farewells to Leonie and left the house as if she hadn't a care in the world, though her eyes were misty with unshed tears. This was the end, the closing of a chapter, and she mustn't give way.

On Monday she went along to the boutique in Pimlico where Sue introduced her to Sally Fairfax, singing her praises loudly.

'But I haven't any experience of selling,' pointed out Marisa. 'It's only fair to tell you that.'

Sally Fairfax frowned consideringly. She was well groomed and smartly dressed with an air of competence not belied by her rather hard mouth.

'That needn't necessarily matter if you're willing to work hard and show an interest in the customers. I can't afford to carry passengers; I've got to make this place pay. Sue tells me that you would want to live in the flat.'

'That's part of the attraction of the job,' said Marisa frankly. 'I want to sell the house I'm living in because it's too big for me, and it's so difficult to find a flat in London at a reasonable rent.'

'Come and look at the accommodation. It's not extensive, but it's adequate.'

The flat consisted of a large bed-sitting-room and a tiny bathroom over the boutique together with a kitchen on the ground floor behind the shop. It was certainly not luxurious, but it was a good deal better than some places Marisa had seen, and by adding one or two pieces of her own furniture she thought she could make it comfortable. Finally it was agreed that she should move into the flat right away since rent-free accommodation counted as part of her salary and Sally wanted to keep her overheads as low as possible.

Marisa moved in that week to find herself quickly falling into her new routine and making a success of the job. Business was brisk and there was so much to keep her occupied that she was glad to be living on the premises. The flat seemed cramped after the spaciousness of the house, while it was a nuisance that the tiny kitchen at the rear of the shop was too small to hold a table or even a breakfast bar so that it meant carrying every meal up the steep flight of stairs and all the dishes down again to wash up. On the other hand she had the minimum of housework to do when she was tired, and she also discovered that she had an unexpected flair for selling, for finding clothes for people which suited them and which they wouldn't regret buying five minutes after they'd left the shop. Sally admitted that she hadn't half Marisa's patience when it came to dealing with an awkward customer, and at the end of the month she said: 'You know, this is definitely your niche. I'm good at buying and you're good at selling, added to which we get on well with each other.'

'Yes, we do,' agreed Marisa.

It had occurred to her that if she really wanted to make a career of the boutique she could suggest a partnership to Sally later on. When she sold the house she would have some capital, and it could be a good idea to invest it in the business. She needed to have an object in life; work was the best antidote to unhappiness and by going to bed tired out each night she managed to sleep.

The following week the estate agent rang to say that he had had a definite offer for the house.

'It's a hundred below our asking price,' said the suave voice on the telephone, 'but this client wouldn't need a mortgage, so there would be no hold-up in that direction. I really think, Miss Farnham, in view of the state of the market, that it might be as well to close with the offer.'

'Yes, I think so too,' agreed Marisa, and by the middle of December the contract had been signed.

Once she had some capital she would have to come to a decision about her future. Should she buy a partnership in the boutique as Sally was urging her to do; did she really want to make the running of it into a career for the next few years at least? Then when she was still dithering Leonie came into the shop just before Christmas. She was looking very smart with her hair newly styled and an attractively striped fur jacket topping her new-length skirt, but she immediately began to plead poverty.

'I wondered if you had anything reasonably priced which I could wear for the wedding,' she said. 'Why on earth Giselle had to choose January, I can't imagine. Spring or summer would have been much easier to dress for.'

'What about one of these new printed velvet dresses?' suggested Marisa. 'It would look very elegant under a fur coat or a jacket.'

She brought out one in tawny shades which Leonie eyed appreciatively.

'Mm, that is rather nice. May I try it on?'

She went into one of the fitting rooms and then called Marisa to see the effect.

'It's such a good fit that I'll take it. I might search for ages in town and not find anything I like so well. Are those French jersey trousers over there?'

'Yes, they're an exclusive line Sally managed to get hold of.'

'Have you my size in beige?'

Leonie chatted while she was trying on the trousers, answering Marisa's questions about Fiona.

'Oh, she's fine now, and loving it at nursery school. Jon's well too, but worried about business like everyone else. He keeps urging me to economise, but I believe in enjoying oneself while one can.'

'And Blake?'

'He's still abroad, coming home just before the wedding. Yes, I'll take the trousers too.'

'Where is the wedding taking place?'

'In the village church at Little Cumming near Leatherhead where Giselle's father has a house—two o'clock on the twentieth. They're going to the Bahamas for the honeymoon. I must say I envy them; I'm pining for the sun again. What are you doing for Christmas, Marisa?'

'I've had an invitation to spend it with friends,' lied Marisa.

'Well, we'd be pleased if you'd drop in for drinks on Christmas morning—any time between eleven and two. I've bribed my daily woman to come in and cook lunch. Her family's grown up, so she doesn't mind.'

When Leonie had gone Sally said: 'I'm glad you've got an invitation for Christmas Day. I was going to suggest that you came along to us.'

'No need for that, but thank you all the same.'

Marisa had no intention of going to the Wantages on Christmas Day in spite of Leonie's invitation. She suspected that she had only been asked out of pity, and decided that it would be just as well to allow the friendship to lapse now. She bought a small chicken which she stuffed, cooked and ate by herself on Christmas Day, following it by fresh fruit salad and cream because she wasn't fond of Christmas pudding.

In spite of a determination to remain cheerful and not feel sorry for herself she was glad when the holiday was over. In the New Year Sally had a sale, more to tempt customers inside than because she had old stock to dispose of. Her sister, who had two small children and was perennially hard up, came to look for bargains and fell for a slinky crêpe dress in emerald green.

'It's just what I need for Bob's office dinner,' she cried. 'All those soft folds will do wonders for my figure. You must let me have it, Sal, it's ages since I was able to afford something really becoming.'

'All right, I'm a fool, I suppose, but you can have it for half price,' said Sally resignedly, 'but it's too long for you. You need at least an inch off it.'

'Your Mrs. Whatsit can fix it for me, can't she? The
139

dinner's on the twenty-first, so I'll pop in on the twentieth and collect the dress.'

'Fine.'

'I'm glad you let Carol have that dress,' said Marisa when Sally's sister had gone. 'It really did suit her.'

'It's true she doesn't get many new clothes these days, but then it was completely irresponsible of her and Bob to start a family at all on his salary. I don't intend to have a baby until Gerry's earning a great deal more than he does now, in fact we may decide to do without children altogether. I don't want to give up the boutique and become immersed in domesticity. I'd rather be a career woman.'

Marisa could appreciate Sally's point of view, but alone in the flat that night she reflected that being a career woman was an arid existence. To her all the money in the world couldn't compensate for the lack of a loving husband and the warmth of family life. Her thoughts went to Giselle whose wedding day was so close at hand. Did she truly love Blake or did she just regard him as a suitable partner, someone who would be a foil for her own talents?

The woman who did Sally's alterations for her took up the hem of the emerald dress, and it was packed ready for Carol to pick up. Then on the morning of the twentieth, just after Marisa had opened up, the telephone rang and Carol's anguished voice wailed: 'Is that you, Sally? Oh, I'm in such an awful mess!'

'No, it's Marisa,' answered Marisa. 'Sally hasn't arrived yet. Can I do anything to help?'

'It's about the green dress I promised to pick up today. I shan't be able to come into town because we've got a burst in the bathroom and I'm waiting for the plumber. Heaven knows when he'll come—you know how dilatory workmen are these days—so it will be quite impossible for me to get away. Tell Sally that she'll have to send the dress out to me instead, will you? I must have it for tomorrow night. I've nothing else to wear.'

Carol's voice sharpened. 'Debbie, come out of that water! Yes, I know it's dripping through the ceiling, that's why I've put the bucket there. Marisa, I'll have to go. Tell Sally not to let me down, please.'

Marisa relayed this news when Sally arrived, and said: 'If there's anything I can do——'

'That's just like Carol,' declared Sally crossly, 'always in a muddle. I know she couldn't help a pipe bursting, but if it hadn't been that it would have been something else. How does she think I'm going to get a dress out to Guildford today? I certainly can't take it myself. Gerry and I are going out this evening, and I've that traveller calling in with that new range of Italian separates. I don't want to miss them.' She hesitated, then went on: 'All the same, I suppose I can't let Carol down. Thursday isn't usually one of our busiest days, so I could spare you, Marisa, if you wouldn't mind going. You can take my car and have the rest of the day off so long as you're back here for half-past five. Would you mind a trip out?'

'No, not at all. I'll pack up the dress and set off.'

The dress was packed in a box, Carol's address supplied together with instructions how to reach it, and Marisa went round to the rear of the premises where Sally's little Renault stood in the yard. She soon manœuvred it out into the road, and drove off in the direction of Guildford. It was a dull, cold day, but fine, and she made good time, finding the avenue where Carol lived without much difficulty.

Carol came to the door with a baby under her arm and a little girl of three at her heels, saying: 'Is that the dress? Thanks a million for bringing it. I knew Sally would find a way of getting it to me.'

'Is there anything I can do?' asked Marisa. 'Has the plumber come?'

'Just, and he says we shall have to have a new hot water tank. Bob will be livid because we've only recently finished paying for repairs to the roof. Would you like to keep an eye on these two for a moment while I make some coffee, that is if you can spare the time?'

'Yes, I can do that. Your sister's given me the rest of

the day off.'

Marisa went into the untidy kitchen and sat with the baby on her knee while Debbie stared solemnly at her. Carol made the coffee, took a cup to the plumber, and then sat chatting to Marisa.

'There's not much I can do here while the water's cut off,' she said, 'so I might as well take the children to the shops. We've known the plumber for years, so I can leave him alone in the house. How do you like working at the boutique?'

'Very much.'

'But you don't intend to make a career of it? You'd opt out if the right man came along?'

'Yes, I would.'

'Like me. Sally can't understand that attitude, but then her marriage has always struck me as a rather cold-blooded affair. Both she and Gerry are ambitious and determined to have the right house in the right area, to meet the right people and so on. Myself, I'd rather have a bit of human warmth and muddle. If Gerry went off with another woman Sally's pride wouldn't allow her to beg him to come back. Now I'd swallow mine willingly if Bob showed signs of straying.' She laughed comfortably. 'Not that he's either the money or the time to have an affair on the side. He's worn out when he comes home at nights, poor lamb.'

The kitchen was cluttered but warm and restful. The baby went to sleep and Debbie played under the table with some bricks, crooning a little song to herself. Marisa relaxed, enjoying the coffee which was surprisingly good, and was sorry when Carol rose reluctantly to say: 'Well, if I'm going to the shops before lunch I'd better make a start. Debbie, come here and let me wash your face.'

'Can I give you a lift into the town?' offered Marisa.

'Thanks, that would be a great help. I'll fetch Tim's pushchair.'

It took considerable effort to get the children packed

into the car, but at last Marisa decanted them all at the shops. When they had waved goodbye she told herself she might as well drive straight back to London, but instead she found herself studying the A.A. map in the side pocket of the car and tracing the route to Little Cumming, which was about ten miles away. The fact that the wedding was fixed for two o'clock would leave time for lunch first if she decided to make the journey. Reason told her that it was the height of folly to give herself the pain of seeing Blake married to Giselle, but she felt compelled to do it. She drove into the country until she saw an attractive pub, then ate a meal of roast lamb and apple tart while she planned her approach to the church.

What she hoped to do was slip in at the back when the ceremony had started, so she deliberately dawdled, reaching the village round about two when all but the bride should be safely in their places. She parked the car by a field gate, then cautiously walked towards the church. There was a line of cars outside the lych-gate and a large limousine was approaching in the distance. Guessing that this held the bride, Marisa darted into the churchyard and positioned herself behind a tree where she could see without being seen.

She was right. The car stopped, and a man got out followed by Giselle. A photographer darted forward and Giselle stood there on her father's arm, her train floating out behind her. She looked poised and completely calm, then when the photographer had finished she turned gracefully and stepped inside the church.

In that moment Marisa almost turned round herself and went back to the car, but something impelled her to walk up the path and enter the church. The choir had preceded the bride up the aisle and were taking their places in the choir stalls, so under cover of this Marisa slipped noiselessly into the back pew, which was empty. She looked mechanically up the aisle to the altar where the bridegroom stood with the best man, her hands involuntarily clenching, then her eyes widened in amazement. The man who turned his head as Giselle reached him was short, dark, and certainly not Blake. It was someone Marisa had never seen before.

CHAPTER IX

She went on staring, sure that her eyes must be playing tricks, then in one of the front pews she caught sight of Blake's back alongside that of Leonie and Jon, and she knew she hadn't been mistaken. Whoever Giselle was marrying it wasn't Blake, but why?

Marisa tiptoed out of the church and walked back to the car, thinking hard all the way. When she had seen the ring on Giselle's finger she had jumped to the wrong conclusion, and Giselle must have known that yet she had remained silent. Was it from jealousy? Had she suspected that Blake cared for Marisa?

A thread of excitement crept up Marisa's spine. When Blake had told her that he owed her an explanation for his conduct before he left Corsica had he been going to tell her that he didn't intend to marry Giselle, that he loved her, Marisa? It didn't seem possible, and yet he had obviously been going to say something important. Oh, if only she hadn't been so flippant, if she had listened to what he had to say, but it was no use lamenting that now. What she must do was try to retrieve the situation—but how? She could hardly go up to him and say: 'When I remarked that Corsica was no more than a pleasant interlude I wasn't aware that you weren't going to marry Giselle', but somehow she had to inform him of the fact.

She started the car and drove back to London, pondering over her problem all the way. Remembering what Carol had said Marisa was prepared to swallow her own pride and ring Blake up, but would he be remaining in England or was he going straight back to Africa after the wedding? A lot depended on that, and finally she decided that her first priority must be to ring Leonie and discover the situation. Her excuse could be an enquiry about the wedding. Leonie would find it quite natural that she should be interested in how the affair had gone off.

There was no point in ringing that night since Leonie and Jon were unlikely to be at home, so Marisa had to contain her impatience until the following day. She found it difficult to fix her attention on her work, and after she had made two mistakes in giving change and spent half an hour looking for a dress which was under her nose Sally enquired: 'What on earth's the matter with you? Are you in love?'

'Sorry, I've got one or two things on my mind,' apologised Marisa, and made a strong effort to concentrate. She was appalled at the way her self-possession had crumbled. She might be reading far too much into that remark of Blake's, and at this rate she would give herself hopelessly away when they met face to face.

She managed to pull herself together, but all the same she was truly thankful when closing time came. She said good night to Sally and went into the kitchen to make herself a cup of tea. Then with it only half drunk she dialled Leonie's number and waited with a rapidly beating heart for the receiver to be picked up. She prayed that Leonie would be at home because she felt she couldn't endure another evening of frustration.

Her prayers were answered. Leonie's voice said: 'Hello,' and Marisa answered: 'It's Marisa. I wondered how the wedding had gone off.'

'Oh, perfectly, as you would expect with Giselle in charge. She looked lovely in wild silk, and of course there were lashings of champagne and everything to eat that you could imagine. A party of us went on to dine and dance at a country club near the village. We didn't get home until three o'clock this morning, so I'm feeling half

145

dead today. I don't know what time Blake would arrive back at his flat. He was very smitten with one of the bridesmaids and took her home after the party broke up.'

For what seemed an endless moment Marisa couldn't speak, then she managed: 'Is he going back to Africa or staying on in England?'

'He's flying back the day after tomorrow, so he's coming to us for a farewell dinner tomorrow night. I've invited Sandra—that's the bridesmaid—as well as another couple, so it should be a good evening. It's high time Blake was settled. I quite thought he intended to marry Giselle, but she told me that they were only good friends and that as soon as she met Denver Howard they fell for each other.'

'I see. I'm glad everything went off successfully. Good-bye, Leonie.'

' 'Bye, Marisa. You must come and see us soon. I'll give you a ring.'

After she had replaced the receiver Marisa sat there staring unseeingly across the room, eventually surfacing to the realisation that she felt both cold and empty. She couldn't eat, but she switched on the electric fire before heating some milk which she drank mechanically. Her only consolation lay in the fact that at least Blake wasn't aware of her feeling for him. She shuddered as she remembered her first impulse to ask Leonie for the number of his flat so that she could ring him there. That embarrassment would have been a thousand times worse than the pain she was suffering now.

But the pain was very real, nevertheless, and afterwards the rest of the evening was only a blur. She went to bed, but it was almost morning before she fell into an exhausted doze. The thought of breakfast was nauseating, but she forced herself to swallow some coffee, and after one look at her pallid face she fished out some blusher and managed to achieve a less wan effect.

Fortunately Sally was too full of her own troubles to speculate on her assistant's. Her car was playing up and since she had been unable to start it and her husband had already left the house she had had to come by bus. She spent some time arranging with a garage to pick the car up, so she had no attention to spare for Marisa, who was thankful for this.

In the early afternoon the telephone rang, and Marisa picked up the receiver only to hear Leonie's voice.

'I've rung to ask a favour,' said Leonie in a rush. 'Look, will you come to dinner tonight? I know it's dreadfully short notice, but that wretched girl Sandra has let me down. She says she's got a cold, but I think she's had a more exciting invitation; perhaps she and Blake didn't click, after all. Anyway, it's left me minus one at the dinner table and five's such an awkward number. Will you be an angel and partner Blake tonight?'

Marisa's first instinct was to say: 'No!' violently and slam down the receiver, but rudeness was foreign to her nature and even while common sense was warning her that she would be foolish to expose herself to heartbreak again and that she ought to put Blake out of her life once and for all she was hesitating.

'Oh, please,' begged Leonie. 'There's no one else I can ask, no one, that is, to whom Blake would be amiable. You know how critical of women he is, but he approves of you.'

'Does he?' said Marisa dubiously, but her heart was beginning to beat faster again while the demon of hope rose once more.

'Of course he does, and I do want him to be in good form. No one can be more charming when he chooses to exert himself, but lately he's been so moody. I didn't think that Giselle announcing her engagement to Denver had affected him much, but when he came back for the wedding he was as grim and silent as if his heart were broken. That was why I was counting on Sandra to make the evening go with a swing. I don't know the other couple terribly well—they're business acquaintances of Jon's—but we owe them hospitality and I thought it would be a good opportunity to pay it off. Do come to my rescue, Marisa.'

'Very well,' agreed Marisa, making up her mind. She was all kinds of a fool, but she would give fate one last chance. She would come face to face with Blake and see what happened. Surely she would be able to tell from his attitude whether he had any feeling for her or not.

'Bless you! The Andersons will pick you up and take you home. They have to come through London, and it won't be much out of their way to pass the boutique. I'll ring Margaret Anderson now and fix things up. See you tonight.'

'What was all that?' enquired Sally. 'You were an age on the phone.'

'Sorry. It was Leonie Wantage, and she wants me to go there to dinner tonight. She's been let down by one of her guests and needs another girl to make up the table.'

'Mm, not exactly flattering, but anything's better than a solitary evening with the radio. What are you going to wear?'

'I haven't thought. My black crêpe, I suppose. It's the only dinner dress I possess.'

'Treat yourself to something out of stock. You can have it at cost.'

Why not? thought Marisa defiantly. It might turn out to be one of the most difficult evenings of her life. She needed the confidence a new dress could give her.

'There's the bronze-green silk jersey,' she ventured.

'The very thing. That unusual shade is immensely flattering. Try it on.'

It fitted perfectly, and the fluid lines made the most of Marisa's slim figure. When the boutique closed that evening she took a bath and made up her face with particular care, smoothing on more eyeshadow than usual and brushing her hair back into a sleek, sophisticated style which complemented the dress. The Andersons were late, and by the time they rang the bell she was suffering qualms and wishing she had refused the invitation, but it was too late to back out, so slinging her velvet jacket round her shoulders she joined them in the car.

Margaret Anderson, plump, pleasant and wearing a dress which was much too fussy, didn't constitute any kind of a rival. She chatted non-stop all the way to Twickenham, dividing her conversation impartially between Marisa and her husband, who was a stocky, silent man. Leonie flung open the door as they arrived, looking supremely elegant in black and white moiré, and told the two women to go into her bedroom to take off their wraps.

When they emerged she was waiting to usher them into the drawing-room where Jon was dispensing drinks.

'Nice to see you, Marisa,' he said. 'What will you have?'

She chose dry sherry, and wondered when Blake would put in an appearance.

As if she had read her thoughts Leonie said: 'Blake rang to say he might be a little delayed. He has several last-minute things to see to since his plane leaves at eleven tomorrow morning.'

'I quite envy him going into all that gorgeous sunshine,' remarked Margaret Anderson brightly, 'especially as the weather here is so wet and cold at present.'

'Sunshine's all very well when you can lounge on a beach all day,' countered her husband, 'but not so enjoyable when you have to do business in the heat.'

The conversation became general, and Marisa strained her ears for the sound of Blake's car. Leonie looked at her watch and said: 'If Blake isn't here in a few moments we shall have to eat without him or everything will be spoiled,' and at that precise second he rang the bell.

When he came into the room Marisa's breathing seemed to be suspended, and she was supremely thankful that he spoke to the Andersons first. Then he turned to her to say in the most matter-of-fact way possible: 'Hallo, Marisa. How are things with you these days?'

She made some commonplace rejoinder, and they all went in to dinner. She had no idea what they ate; she was only aware of Blake and of the fact that he looked thinner. Otherwise he was exactly the same as he had always been, and she was filled with a dreadful certainty that she had been mistaken in ever thinking that he had wanted a deeper relationship with her.

Because she was sitting next to him and she couldn't stay mum she forced herself to make conversation, and in a reckless attempt to contribute to the gaiety of the evening drank a third glass of wine. It had the effect of loosening her tongue, and presumably she sounded quite witty, because the others laughed a lot and the evening passed more quickly than she had dared to hope.

It was just as well she wasn't longing to get him to herself, because there was no chance of it. He didn't even sit on the sofa beside her as Leonie had indicated, but stayed on his feet in the drawing-room passing coffee cups and brandy glasses until Jon dropped down next to her to tell her that Fiona had started dancing class and was loving it. Then the talk centred on Africa and Blake described the dry heat of the desert until she could almost feel it, and in spite of herself she couldn't conceal her interest.

Time wore on and at last Margaret Anderson said: 'I hate to break up the party, but we really must be going. Are you ready, Marisa?'

'Yes, of course.' Marisa rose to her feet. 'I'll get my jacket.'

'Don't bother,' said Leonie. 'I'm going up to the bedroom with Margaret and I'll bring it down for you.'

'And I'll get that road map you were asking about,' remarked Jon to Paul Anderson, and the two of them disappeared.

For the first time that evening Marisa and Blake were alone together. Her hands were clammy but her mouth was dry, and she couldn't think of a single thing to say.

'I hope you have a good journey tomorrow,' she brought out at last, and he answered indifferently: 'It's very boring. I usually sleep most of the time.'

The seconds ticked away, and she had the agonising

conviction that this was the last time she would see him. He was looking down, and she noticed the taut angle of his jaw and the new lines round his mouth. He was definitely thinner and more strained than when she had seen him last. His job would be an exacting one, of course, and it couldn't be easy working in all that heat. Her love for him rose up in a great wave, and before she could stop herself she'd blurted out: 'I thought you were going to marry Giselle.'

He looked up and stared at her. 'What gave you that impression?'

Somewhere a telephone began to ring and then was silenced.

Marisa was already regretting that she had spoken. 'It seemed so obvious.'

'But surely—'

Jon appeared at the door. 'Blake, you're wanted on the telephone. An urgent message, by the sound of it.'

'Will you excuse me?'

Blake vanished as Margaret Anderson came in followed by her husband and Leonie.

'Well, I'm ready at last. Say goodbye to Blake for me, will you, Leonie. I don't want to interrupt him.'

'He's likely to be ages on the telephone. Since he took over from Royce Lambert he's scarcely had a moment to call his own.'

Her goodbyes said, Marisa settled into the back of the Andersons' car. The warming effect of the wine and the brandy she had drunk with her coffee had evaporated, and she felt tired and depressed. When the Andersons dropped her at the boutique she invited them in, but was thankful they refused. She fixed her mind on hot milk and going straight to bed. If only she could fall asleep quickly things mightn't look so bad in the morning.

She took two aspirins with the milk and clutching a hot water bottle got into bed. In spite of her wretchedness this combination soon sent her off until she was wakened by the pealing of the shop door bell. She blinked incredulously at her bedside clock, which gave the time as twelve-thirty, only half an hour since she had got into bed, and then as the bell went on ringing she groped for her dressing gown and slippers.

'All right,' she muttered as she ran downstairs, 'I'm coming!'

She could only think that it must be the police, that perhaps the shop had been broken into and they were rousing her to tell her of this. She groped her way to the door and unlocked it, fully expecting when she opened it to see a man in uniform. Instead it was Blake who stood there, and she gaped at him in astonishment.

'It's you!' she gasped. 'What—what's the matter?'

'I must talk to you.'

'But it's nearly one o'clock in the morning.'

'I don't care what time it is,' he said violently. 'I'm coming in.'

She moved aside, conscious that she was clutching her dressing gown round her and that her hair was standing on end.

'Couldn't you have waited until tomorrow?' she asked feebly. 'That is, today.'

'No, I couldn't; I've a plane to catch, remember? Look, you can't stand in this draughty place. Isn't there somewhere we can switch on a fire?'

'We'll have to go upstairs. There's no room to sit down in the kitchen.'

She led the way up to her bed-sitting-room, and knelt down to switch on the electric fire.

'That's better,' said Blake. He pulled a blanket off the bed and handed it to her. 'Wrap that round you and sit down. Now I want an explanation of that cryptic remark you made just before you left this evening. You are the most exasperating female I've ever known! To come out with that and then disappear! Why the devil didn't you wait until I'd finished on the telephone?'

'The Andersons were ready to go, and anyway, there didn't seem much point in it,' said Marisa numbly. 'You scarcely spoke to me all evening.'

'I didn't get much chance. You were the life and soul of the party. However, I didn't come out here at this hour to be sidetracked. You haven't answered my question. What made you believe I was going to marry Giselle?'

'When we were in Corsica it seemed so obvious—and Leonie hinted—then when Giselle was wearing an engagement ring naturally I thought that you and she——'

'But didn't Giselle tell you that she was marrying Howard?'

'I said something to her about congratulating you and she let me go on believing——'

Marisa stopped dead, realising all at once the conclusion Blake might draw. But it was too late.

'Go on,' he said softly. 'Giselle allowed you to continue thinking that she was engaged to me. Now why would she do that?'

'She probably thought it was a tremendous joke,' said Marisa desperately. 'Blake, I'm tired and this conversation isn't getting us anywhere. Please go.'

'On the contrary, it's told me exactly what I wanted to know. Giselle deceived you because she was jealous of you, because she knew that I'd fallen in love with you and all along she was determined to spoil things for you if she could. I had my suspicions about her attitude that day in Porto when Fiona fell down the cliff. Giselle knew perfectly well that you'd gone to the shop and she wanted you to be blamed for Fiona's disappearance, though I think she was frightened by what actually happened. Unfortunately you played right into her hands both times. Didn't Leonie mention Howard's name when she was talking about the engagement?'

'I never really gave her the chance.' Marisa was staring at him incredulously. 'What did you say about falling in love?'

'That I fell in love with you in Corsica, much against my will, I may add. I had my life all nicely mapped out, and marriage wasn't included in my scheme for some while yet. Up to then I'd had a vague idea that some time in the future probably Giselle and I would make a match of it simply because it would have been so convenient, but there didn't seem to be any hurry. Then you came along, and though I didn't approve of you at first, gradually I found I couldn't put you out of my mind.

'When we went up to the mountain village together I realised for the first time I was beginning to care deeply for you, but I had to rush back to England and then the practice engulfed me and I hadn't a moment to call my own. Royce Lambert decided to retire and asked me if I'd like to buy him out. I agreed, but he wasn't in a fit state to conduct negotiations, so Giselle had to act as go-between. It was then I let her see that there was no longer any question of a marriage between us and in her chagrin she couldn't conceal her jealousy of you. Not that I flatter myself she was ever desperately in love with me, but she'd decided I was a suitable partner and her pride was galled by my rejection.'

He sounded so calm about it all that Marisa felt her temper rise.

'It couldn't have been a lasting blow; she soon settled for someone else,' she pointed out belligerently.

'Oh, Howard had been in the background for some time. He's successful, rich and dull. Giselle will keep him right under her thumb and they'll probably be very happy. You and I, of course, are an entirely different proposition.'

'Are we?'

'Yes, we are, my darling.' Blake grinned at her and Marisa's annoyance vanished while joy bubbled through her veins like champagne.

His arms came round her and they were locked together in a kiss which roused depths within her which she had never suspected existed. When she surfaced again she said foolishly: 'I can't believe it—that you care for me, I mean. I realise that you left Corsica in too great a hurry to say anything, but why didn't you write to me when you got back to England?'

'Because I literally hadn't a minute to myself, and when I returned to the flat at nights I was too dog-tired to express myself properly on paper. I could have telephoned, but that would have been equally unsatisfactory. I wanted to discuss things face to face, and I believed that when we could be together you'd understand why I'd waited. As soon as Royce was mending I had to fly to East Africa to fulfil our contract there, but I determined to return home for Fiona's birthday and to see you then. You know what happened to upset my plans.'

'To bolster my pride I pretended that the kiss in Corsica meant nothing to me.'

'It wasn't true, was it?'

'No,' admitted Marisa honestly. 'I'd begun to care for you some while before that, but I thought you were committed to Giselle, and your remark about having come home to see her didn't persuade me otherwise.'

'If only I'd known that was the trouble! As it was I thought you were indifferent to me, and it was a hell of a jolt. Never give me such a fright again.'

As his lips sought her throat he pulled her down into the largest armchair, and she relaxed in the ecstasy of his lovemaking. Finally she said reluctantly: 'Darling, you'll have to go. You must get some sleep before your journey tomorrow.'

'I suppose you're right.'

Blake rose to his feet and looked down at her. The expression in his eyes made her blink back the tears. To her he had always appeared so self-assured; she had never dreamed he could look so vulnerable.

She smiled up at him. 'When you're home again we'll have plans to make.'

'I suppose you'll want a big wedding,' he said wryly. 'Don't make me wait too long, will you?'

'I've no one to invite to a big wedding, so I'll settle for Leonie and Jon—and you and me.'

'You mean it?'

155

'What do the trappings matter if we can be together for always? Heavens, doesn't that sound corny?'

'It sounds too good to be true, my love, but I'll hold you to it. Now I'm going, but I'll pick you up here at half-past nine tomorrow morning, and on the way to the airport we'll work out a few things. You can drive yourself back in my car and have the use of it while I'm away.'

He gave her one last hard kiss, then ran downstairs. Marisa heard the shop door click behind him as she crept back to bed. The sheets were icy and her hot water bottle had gone cold, but she was bathed in a warm glow of happiness. There were bound to be ups and downs in marriage and she and Blake would probably quarrel violently from time to time, but as long as they had each other she felt she could weather anything. With a sigh of fulfilment she snuggled down and fell soundly asleep.

that's Entertain-ment!

Harlequin

the unique monthly magazine packed with good things for Harlequin readers!

A Complete Harlequin Novel

You'll get hours of reading enjoyment from Harlequin fiction. Along with a variety of specially selected short stories, every issue of the magazine contains a complete romantic novel.

Readers' Page

A lively forum for exchanging news and views from Harlequin readers. If you would like to share your thoughts, we'd love to hear from you.

Arts and Crafts

Unusual handicraft articles are a fascinating feature of Harlequin magazine. You'll enjoy making your own gifts and indulging your creativity when you use these always clear and easy-to-follow instructions.

Author's Own Story . . .

Now, meet the very real people who create the romantic world of Harlequin! In these unusual author profiles a well-known author tells you her own personal story.

Harlequin Cookery

Temptingly delicious dishes, plain and fancy, from all over the world. Recreate these dishes from tested, detailed recipes, for your family and friends.

Faraway Places . . .

Whether it's to remind you of places you've enjoyed visiting, or to learn about places you're still hoping to see, you'll find the travel articles informative and interesting — and just perfect for armchair travelling.

Harlequin

An annual subscription to the magazine — 12 issues — costs just $9.00.
Look for the order form on the next page.